AN AMISH CHRISTMAS GIFT

A SHORT STORY

(INCLUDES AMISH RECIPES)

BETH WISEMAN

Published in Fayetteville, Texas, United States.

Cover Design: Elizabeth Wiseman Mackey

Note: This novel is a work of fiction. Names, characters, places, and incidents are either products of the author's imagination or used fictitiously. All characters are fictional, and any similarity to people living or dead is purely coincidental.

To Diana and Terry

ACCLAIM FOR OTHER BOOKS BY BETH WISEMAN

The House That Love Built

"This sweet story with a hint of mystery is touching and emotional. Humor sprinkled throughout balances the occasional seriousness. The development of the love story is paced perfectly so that the reader gets a real sense of the characters." ~ ROMANTIC TIMES, 4-STAR REVIEW

"[The House That Love Built] is a warm, sweet tale of faith renewed and families restored." ~ BOOKPAGE

Need You Now

"Wiseman, best known for her series of Amish novels, branches out into a wider world in this story of family, dependence, faith, and small-town Texas, offering a character for every reader to relate to . . . With an enjoyable cast of outside characters, *Need You Now* breaks the molds of small-town stereotypes. With issues ranging from special education and teen cutting to what makes a marriage strong, this is a compelling and worthy read." ~ BOOKLIST

"Wiseman gets to the heart of marriage and family interests in a way that will resonate with readers, with an intricately written plot featuring elements that seem to be ripped from current headlines. God provides hope for Wiseman's characters even in the most desperate situations." ~ ROMANTIC TIMES, 4-STAR REVIEW

"Wiseman gets to the heart of marriage and family issues in a way that will resonate with readers . . ." ~ ROMANTIC TIMES

"With issues ranging from special education and teen cutting to what makes a marriage strong, this is a compelling and worthy read." ~ BOOKLIST

"You may think you are familiar with Beth's wonderful story-telling gift but this is something new! This is a story that will stay with you for a long, long time. It's a story of hope when life seems hopeless. It's a story of how God can redeem the seemingly unredeemable. It's a message the Church, the world needs to hear." ~ SHEILA WALSH, AUTHOR OF *GOD LOVES BROKEN PEOPLE*

"Beth Wiseman tackles these difficult subjects with courage and grace. She reminds us that true healing can only come by being vulnerable and honest before our God who loves us more than anything." ~ DEBORAH

BEDFORD, BESTSELLING AUTHOR OF *HIS OTHER WIFE, A ROSE BY THE DOOR, AND THE PENNY* (COAUTHORED WITH JOYCE MEYER)

The Land of Canaan Novels

"Wiseman's voice is consistently compassionate and her words flow smoothly." ~ PUBLISHERS WEEKLY REVIEW OF *SEEK ME WITH ALL YOUR HEART*

"Wiseman's third Land of Canaan novel overflows with romance, broken promises, a modern knight in shining armor and hope at the end of the rainbow." ~ ROMANTIC TIMES

"In *Seek Me with All Your Heart*, Beth Wiseman offers readers a heart-warming story filled with complex characters and deep emotion. I instantly loved Emily, and eagerly turned each page, anxious to learn more about her past—and what future the Lord had in store for her." ~ SHELLEY SHEPARD GRAY, BESTSELLING AUTHOR OF *THE SEASONS OF SUGARCREEK SERIES*

"Wiseman has done it again! Beautifully compelling, *Seek Me with All Your Heart* is a heart-warming story of faith, family, and renewal. Her characters and descriptions are captivating, bringing the story to life with the turn of every page." ~ AMY CLIPSTON, BESTSELLING AUTHOR OF *A GIFT OF GRACE*

The Daughters of the Promise Novels

"Well-defined characters and story make for an enjoyable read." ~ ROMANTIC TIMES REVIEW OF *PLAIN PURSUIT*

"A touching, heartwarming story. Wiseman does a particularly great job of dealing with shunning, a controversial Amish practice that seems cruel and unnecessary to outsiders . . . If you're a fan of Amish fiction, don't miss *Plain Pursuit!*" ~ KATHLEEN FULLER, AUTHOR OF *THE MIDDLEFIELD FAMILY NOVELS.*

OTHER BOOKS BY BETH
WISEMAN

Contemporary Women's Fiction
   The House that Love Built
   Need You Now
   The Promise

Daughters of the Promise Series
   Plain Perfect
   Plain Pursuit
   Plain Promise
   Plain Paradise
   Plain Proposal
   Plain Peace

Land of Canaan Series
   Seek Me With All Your Heart
   The Wonder of Your Love
   His Love Endures Forever

Amish Secrets Series

Her Brothers Keeper
Love Bears All Things
Home All Along

Amish Journeys Series
Hearts in Harmony
Listening to Love
A Beautiful Arrangement

An Amish Inn Series
A Picture of Love
An Unlikely Match
A Season of Change

An Amish Bookstore Series
The Bookseller's Promise
The Story of Love
Hopefully Ever After

Stand-Alone Amish Novel
The Amish Matchmakers

Short Stories/Novellas
An Amish Adoption
The Messenger
Return of the Monarchs

Surf's Up Novellas
A Tide Worth Turning
Message In A Bottle
The Shell Collector's Daughter

Christmas by the Sea

Collections

Memoir

GLOSSARY

ach: oh

daed: dad

danki: thank you

Englisch: those who are not Amish; the English language

Gott: God

gut: good

haus: house

kaffi: coffee

kinner: children

lieb: love

maed: girl

mamm: mom

mei: my

mudder: mother

nee: no

Ordnung: written and unwritten rules in an Amish district

rumschpringe: running around time for teenagers, beginning at 16 years old

Ya: yes

CHAPTER 1

*H*annah King wished she could skip Christmas this year even though she'd always treasured the holiday and everything it represented. She forced herself to wrap gifts while her children spent time at their aunt and uncle's house on this crisp December morning. The aroma of freshly baked bread hung in the air, orange embers crackled as they shimmied up the fireplace, and she'd organized the children's presents from where she sat on her living room floor—just like she'd done every year. She was surrounded by various rolls of wrapping paper, colorful bows she'd made from ribbon purchased at the market, and an assortment of boxes.

As was tradition, they wouldn't have a Christmas tree, but Hannah would place the wrapped gifts around the living room to create a festive atmosphere. She'd already laid out garland atop the fireplace mantel and placed poinsettias on either side of the stone structure while her two daughters helped decorate other areas. Lillian, who had just turned seven, had attached red bows on the porch columns outside and created a lovely centerpiece for the dining room table using pinecones, red and green ribbons, and holly. Eighteen-year-old Mae had unpacked other decorations they kept stored in the basement and placed them around the house. Hannah hoped that being with her sister's family for the day might infuse some holiday joy into her daughters' lives.

Ruth and Henry didn't have children of their own yet, and they doted on Hannah's girls. Spoiled them was more like it. And that was okay with Hannah. It was their first Christmas without Paul, her beloved husband and father of the two beautiful girls. A life taken much too early.

Hannah slipped the pink sweater she'd knitted for Lillian into a box. Her youngest daughter could still get away with wearing pastel colors at her age, and pink was Lillian's favorite color. She chose red and white striped wrapping paper, but she hadn't even closed the box when she covered her face with both hands and cried, the type of sobbing that people do only when they are alone. Her grief shook her to the core and often came on unexpectedly. Hannah did her best to stay strong for Lillian and Mae and never showed her emotions around them. She hadn't cried in front of anyone since the funeral, not even her sister, to whom she'd always been close. It was her job, as a mother, to be strong for her girls, and feigning strength around everyone else was good practice, albeit difficult.

Today, she needed the release, and shipping the girls to Ruth and Henry was about more than just needing privacy to wrap presents. She needed the solitude to let go of some of the grief that had such a firm hold on her, a type of suffocation that left her feeling as though she couldn't breathe sometimes. Hopefully, she could get it out of her system before the girls returned. It had been six months since the accident that took her husband's life at only forty-one years old. She couldn't help but wonder if she would always feel the stabbing pain in her chest that represented the void in her life.

MAE ENJOYED BEING with her Aunt Ruth and Uncle Henry. Even though they had loved her father, she supposed it was easier for them to get on with life than it was for Mae, her sister, and her mother. There was a giant hole in their hearts, and even with all the Christmas decorations at home, the absence of their father, the void, the changes, the sadness . . . it hovered in the air like a dark cloud that would never produce rain or go away. The worst part was hearing her mother crying herself to sleep every night, only to pretend everything was okay when she was around Mae and her sister. Lillian was only seven and didn't have as many memories to hold onto as Mae. But after twenty years of marriage, it was her mother who seemed to be suffering the most, and it scared Mae.

Amish funerals were a sober affair but showing grief in public was discouraged. As was tradition, Mae's father had been buried three days after his death. Preceding the burial, a viewing was held at their home, followed by a church service, and then her father was laid to rest in the Amish cemetery, his headstone identical to all the others.

Mae's mother had remained stoic and hadn't cried throughout any of the services even though Lillian and Mae shed tears, along with several others. Maybe her mother should have let go of some of her emotions. Was all that grief bottled up inside and spilling out privately at night? How long would her mother suffer? *Forever?*

Mae stood at the window and watched her uncle push Lillian on the swing when her aunt came up beside her.

"How's your *mamm?*" Aunt Ruth was three years younger than her mother, a beautiful woman with auburn hair and green eyes. She told everyone she must be adopted because there wasn't a redhead anywhere in the family tree. Mae's grandparents laughed at the notion and assured everyone Ruth wasn't adopted.

"She's okay." Mae hadn't told anyone that she often heard her mother softly crying late at night. With each new day, she prayed that her mom wouldn't suffer so much. Even though she fought hard to hide it, Mae could see the sadness in her mother's eyes, her daily interactions, and especially during worship service. Maybe the Spirit moved her. Perhaps she begged God to bring back her husband and Lillian and Mae's father.

Her Aunt Ruth put a hand on her back, rubbing gently. "I know it doesn't feel like it right now, but time will ease the pain, and eventually you will all be happy again." She paused, sighing. "Your *daed* was a *gut* man."

Mae's bottom lip trembled. She wasn't as good as her mother when it came to hiding her emotions.

"Look at those two." Aunt Ruth lowered her arm from Mae's back and pointed out the window. "He's going to make a wonderful *daed* someday."

Coming here was an escape from the sadness at her house, and her aunt must have sensed that Mae didn't want to talk about the loss they'd suffered.

Her aunt and uncle had been trying to have a baby for over ten years. There was no medical reason they shouldn't be able to, according to the doctor. Mae had heard about fertility drugs and in vitro fertilization, but most of their people—her aunt and uncle included—believed conception was in God's hands. "And you'll be a wonderful *mudder*," Mae said as she turned to her and smiled.

"We will see." Aunt Ruth spoke with an air of hope marred by a dose of doubt as she grabbed Mae's hand and led her toward the kitchen. "Since we have some time to ourselves, I want to hear about this new boyfriend you have. I mean, I've known the Byler's for years, but it seems like Johnny turned into a man overnight." She pulled out a kitchen chair and motioned for Mae to sit. "I'll pour us some *kaffi*, and I made banana bread this morning."

"He goes by John now, not Johnny." Mae reached for a slice of warm bread after her aunt set two plates and a platter on the table, then she returned with two cups of coffee.

"Your *mamm* said you two are spending a lot of time together." She smiled. "Do you think *John* is the one?"

Mae had gone out with two other boys after she'd turned sixteen and her parents allowed her to date. Each relationship had only lasted a few months and never progressed past a kiss on the cheek. John was different, and deep inside, Mae knew he was the one for her. She'd known him all her life, but his family lived outside of

Montgomery. The town in southern Indiana was small, but John, his parents, and siblings were still part of the same district as Mae and her family. But due to the distance between their homes, she hadn't really gotten to know him until he began working at the lumberyard near her house. They had been seeing each other for three months, ever since she'd gone to the lumberyard to pick up supplies for small repairs needed on their house. She and John had slipped into an easy conversation, and before she left, he had asked her out for supper.

"I don't know if he is the one." Mae swallowed hard. She disliked lying to anyone, especially someone she loved as much as Aunt Ruth. But telling her aunt the truth would cause more heartache for everyone. Mae had already let things get out of hand with John. "We haven't been seeing each other all that long."

Her aunt got a faraway look in her eyes, then smiled as she refocused on Mae. "I knew I *liebed* Henry and that he was the one for me by our third date."

Mae longed to tell her aunt that she'd fallen for John right away, too, but she only forced a smile. "I guess we will see how it goes."

Her aunt took a bite of bread, then dabbed her mouth with her napkin. "When do you see him again?"

"Tonight. He's coming over." Mae's heart fluttered at the thought. Her mother would put Lillian to bed early, then disappear into her bedroom so Mae and John could sit on the couch in the living room and have some time alone. She appreciated her mother's efforts.

"It's supposed to snow." Aunt Ruth lifted her shoulders, grinning, as she clutched her coffee cup between her hands. "So romantic. A warm fire, maybe some hot cider, and your *mamm* will have the house decorated for Christmas. It sounds wonderful."

Mae envisioned the evening, and it would be exactly as her aunt described. She hoped she wouldn't hear her mother crying in her bedroom. She prayed that thoughts of her father wouldn't overtake her emotions and cloud the evening. Grief had stages. She'd read a book about it that Aunt Ruth had given her. Mae knew time would heal her, but she wasn't sure that was the case for her mother, who seemed stuck in a bad place, unable to get past the intense pain, evidenced by her unwillingness to even mention Mae's father and crying herself to sleep almost every night. She did her best to put on a good act during daylight hours by attempting to be cheerful, and Mae was pretty sure her younger sister bought into it, but Mae didn't. For a while, she had thought her mother was getting better. Or her mother had just been better at hiding her emotions during those interludes. Perhaps the holidays had caused her grief to resurface even more.

She forced the thoughts away and cleared her throat. "John is a wonderful man," she finally said in response to her aunt's comments. But she would lose him to another woman eventually because Mae had no plans to marry John Byler.

CHAPTER 2

*J*ohn cranked up the battery-operated heater in his buggy, pulled his black coat snug around him before he took hold of the reins and backed up, anxious to arrive at Mae's house. She'd have a warm fire going, coffee or hot cider ready, and she'd already told him they had been decorating for Christmas. He wouldn't care if they met in a rundown barn in the woods if he was near her. Being in her arms was all the warmth he needed. But the ambiance she'd described would be the perfect setting for tonight since John had a special surprise for Mae.

Snow swirled in powdery circles like magic fairy dust leading him to his future wife. It was much too soon to propose, but he knew beyond a shadow of a doubt that Mae was the woman he wanted to marry then raise a family. Six children. Three boys and three girls. He smiled to himself as he pictured Mae and their children seated around a big table in the house John would build for them. He'd already purchased a two-acre tract for when the time came to build a home. He'd been saving his money since he'd started working at sixteen, for only two years, but it had been enough to put a down payment on the property.

He spent the rest of his journey daydreaming about the life he and Mae would have. Hopefully, next fall, after the harvest, they would get married.

Everything was blanketed in white by the time he arrived at Mae's house almost forty-five minutes later. He was used to the long buggy ride to work daily. It would have been easier to go straight from work to Mae's house, but he had chores to do at home before he could visit her in the evenings, which made for a lot of traveling. But he'd travel however far he had to so that he could spend time with her.

After he pulled on his black knit cap, he stepped out of the buggy and unhitched his horse, then led the stallion to the lean-to nearby. Mae had already put out fresh oats and water for the animal.

Dodging the snowfall put a spring in John's step as he jogged toward the house with his chin tucked and gloved hands cupped above his eyebrows. His breath clouded in front of him, but it was impossible not to notice the evening light reflecting off the flakes that created a vibrant landscape.

He was stepping out of his boots on the covered front porch when Mae opened the door, smiling.

John was sure his future bride grew more beautiful with each passing day. Her light brown hair was tucked beneath her prayer covering. She'd told him it had grown past her waist, although he wouldn't see the long tresses until they were married. Maybe before, if they went swimming over the summer, or if she allowed him to see her hair down. Some Amish women, his mother being one of them, didn't reveal their hair until marriage. Others were more liberal about the tradition. John wasn't sure what Mae's feelings were on the subject.

"Hurry and get out of your coat. You must be freezing." She bounced up on her toes as she hugged herself to stay warm from the cold air he was letting in.

He slid out of his coat and shook it before draping it over his arm, then popped off his hat and gloves, shaking off as much snow as he could before crossing the threshold to hang the items on the rack inside.

Mae closed the door behind him, then gave him a quick hug. He glanced around the living room filled with holiday decorations as the smell of cinnamon filled his nostrils. They made their way to the fireplace, where he warmed his hands, anxious to cup her cheeks and gaze into her brown eyes before kissing her the way he had been for the past two months. Their first month together had consisted of hugs and kisses on the cheek, but things had evolved into more than a close friendship. They had shared their first passionate kiss behind the barn after worship service at the Lantz's house. He had longed to be in her arms from that moment on. She stayed in his heart and on his mind even when he wasn't with her.

He was glad to be alone with Mae. Lillian was most likely already in bed. But Hannah, Mae's mother, could be nearby. She mostly stayed to herself in her bedroom when John visited, but he wasn't going to kiss Mae until he knew for sure.

"*Mamm* is already in her bedroom," Mae said as she grinned. "She said to tell you hello."

John rubbed his hands together to make sure they were warm enough, then wasted no more time before he cupped Mae's cheeks, his eyes fixed on hers. Could she read his expression? Did she know how much he loved her? They hadn't said the words, but he could feel the intensity of her emotions when he covered her mouth with his in a kiss that always left him weak in the knees.

Tonight was the night . . . that John would tell Mae that he was in love with her.

MAE WAS LOST in the euphoria of John's tender embrace, the way he held her face in his strong hands, and the exploratory way that he kissed her repeatedly. The crackling of the fire fueled the warmth in her heart, and she wished she could live in this moment forever.

Because it couldn't last.

She loved him so much it hurt sometimes, and when she wasn't with him, she longed to see him. It was a cross between agony and euphoria She was pretty sure he felt the same way but admitting it to each other would change things. It would feel like a commitment. Maybe they were already emotionally committed but saying it aloud would solidify a future that Mae could only dream about.

She eased out of his arms, kissed him tenderly on the cheek, then nodded to the coffee table. "I've got hot cider and cinnamon rolls."

"Those look delicious. And the decorations are beautiful too."

"*Danki*. Now let's get some food in you."

On the nights he visited her, he confessed to missing supper with his family, saying he was anxious to get on the road to see her. Most of the Amish families Mae knew, hers included, ate their evening meal at five o'clock. She'd repeatedly asked him to come for supper and that they could eat later those nights. He insisted it would be too late for all of them to eat since he had to work until five. After traveling home and handling his chores, he didn't arrive at her house until almost seven, sometimes later. Mae had offered to heat up leftovers for him, also, but he said he just wanted to focus his attention solely on her. She always made sure to have plenty of snacks though.

After they were settled on the couch, he took a big bite of cinnamon roll. "These are the best I've ever had," he said after he'd swallowed.

Mae chuckled. "You say that about everything me or *Mamm* make for you to eat." She imagined all the meals they could share together if they were to get married and have a family, something she used to think she wanted.

When he rubbed his stomach and smiled, an indication he was full after eating four large cinnamon rolls, Mae picked up their plates. Sometimes, she had finger sandwiches or snacks, but John had a fondness for anything freshly baked and didn't mind having it for supper. It was a long ride for him to visit her, and she appreciated the fact he had repeatedly told her that he didn't mind making the journey. She at least wanted to make sure he left with a full tummy . . . even if it was cinnamon rolls or a finger food.

Her relationship with John had begun as a distraction for Mae. Not that she wasn't wildly attracted to him, but she'd feared the grief over losing her father would leave her never feeling happy again. No one could fill the void of losing her dad, but John provided her with an escape. She had never meant to fall in love with him.

She held her breath as the clock in the kitchen ticked, trying to hear if her mother was crying in the bedroom, but she probably wouldn't hear her from the kitchen. As badly as Mae felt, the loss of her father seemed to have paralyzed her mother emotionally, even though she tried not to show it in front of her daughters. In some ways, there was just a shell of her mother left, a woman who went through the life she was expected to live, but like a robot who didn't express emotion. It wasn't that Hannah King wasn't a good mother to her children, but she was absent. Gone. Like Mae and Lillian's father but in a different way.

She refocused on John when she rounded the corner and came back to the living room. Could he be any more handsome? His dark hair was cut in the traditional style. She'd heard the English call it a bowl cut but John's bangs were long and pushed to the side, and he had what the Amish called 'hat hair' from where his hat had been on his head all day. But it was his dark eyes that Mae could get lost in, and with only the light from the lantern and the glow of the fire, gold flecks twinkled in his brown eyes and grew brighter as he grew closer.

John Byler wasn't just handsome. He truly cared about people, and it showed in his everyday actions. Since Mae had been around him, she'd seen him carry an elderly

English woman's bags to her car when she struggled with the weight of her purchases at the lumberyard. He'd given a homeless man twenty dollars after his friend advised him against it, saying the man might just use it to buy alcohol or drugs. John's response was, "Or food." Then he just smiled.

His tenderness extended much further than strangers and was apparent the most when he was around his loved ones. John had a large family, and Mae knew all of them since they attended the same worship services. She liked to think her people were good in nature overall, but John seemed to take his goodness to another level, and she loved that about him.

As he put an arm around her, snuggling closer, Mae wondered if her father would have approved of them being alone together in the living room. *Probably not.* But Mae suspected her mother would have convinced him that Mae was responsible and that John could be trusted.

Mae missed her mother.

In between snacking on cinnamon rolls and sipping cider, they chatted about their day. John had spent the afternoon doing inventory at the lumberyard, and Mae told him about her visit with her aunt and uncle. Then John became unusually quiet, wringing his hands together.

Slowly he turned to her, tucked a strand of loose hair behind her ear, nuzzled her neck, then gently brushed his lips against hers before they locked eyes.

"I have something to tell you, Mae King." He kissed the tip of her nose, and Mae stopped breathing. If it was what she thought it would be, then their time together would be coming to an end soon. "I can't hold it in any longer," he said in a whisper, the fire continuing to crackle, the clock ticking louder in Mae's mind.

Please don't. He would expect her to say it back, and she couldn't.

He gently took her cheeks into his hands and gazed into her eyes. "Mae, I—"

She crushed her lips to his, causing their foreheads to knock together. Any discomfort from their heads bumping was quickly dissipating as Mae kissed him with all the passion she felt. Because she knew it would be the last time.

He eased her away and captured her eyes again as he tenderly clutched her shoulders. "Mae, I *lieb* you. I know we're young, and I know we've only been seeing each other for three months, but I am sure I am in *lieb* with you."

Mae chewed on her bottom lip as she avoided his eyes, casting them down as she reached up and twirled the string of her prayer covering. She couldn't ignore him, and when she finally looked into his eyes, she saw his fear . . . fear that she didn't feel the same way.

"*Danki,*" she finally said barely above a whisper. "That's nice of you to say," she added when his jaw dropped slightly, his eyes searching hers.

She stood abruptly. "Uh, I think I hear Lillian awake in her room. I should probably go check on her." It was a lie she would ask God to forgive later.

John slowly lifted himself from the couch and looped his thumbs beneath his suspenders. "*Ya,* I should probably go. It's getting late."

It wasn't late, and he didn't look at her as he moved toward the door and quickly dressed in his coat, hat, and gloves.

Mae could feel her heart cracking. But this was the kindest thing to do for John, to let him move on and fall in love with someone who wanted to have a life with him. He was right . . . they were young. They would both get over this even though the pain in Mae's chest felt unbearable, and she hoped she could hold off her tears until he was gone.

At the door, he kissed her on the cheek. "Bye, Mae."

"Bye," she mouthed, aware that no sound came out.

After the door between them closed, she pressed her head to the wood and laid her hands flat against the surface on either side of her head. She didn't want to cry, but tears spilled down her cheeks just the same.

Then she heard a familiar sound coming from her mother's bedroom. Quiet whimpering.

Mae wanted to burst through her mother's bedroom door, climb into bed with her, and hold her tightly, to comfort her. Maybe it should be the other way around, but as badly as Mae was hurting, it was worse for her mother. Mae was never going to allow herself to love the way her mother had loved her father. She'd never survive the pain if she lost a husband, and she'd end up in constant agony like her mother.

She padded up the stairs, stopping to check on Lillian who was sound asleep, then she ran to her room and waited until she was behind her bedroom door before she pressed her face into her pillow and sobbed.

CHAPTER 3

*J*ohn felt like he'd been punched in the gut the entire way home, his stomach twisting and churning with humiliation. How could he have misread Mae's feelings for him and embarrassed himself the way he did? He would have never told her he loved her if he hadn't been sure of her feelings. But he'd been wrong, and the awkwardness of the exchange made him not want to face her ever again, which would be impossible. He would see her at least twice a month at worship service. He doubted she would visit him at the lumberyard anymore or invite him to her house. Her flushed face and the way she'd avoided his eyes expressed how uncomfortable his admission had been for her.

By the time he got home, he had a knot in his throat the size of a walnut. He couldn't remember the last time he'd cried, but his eyes were moist as he made his way up the porch steps, praying his parents and three sisters were asleep. If anyone spoke to him right now, he feared he couldn't mask his emotions, and that would top off his already humiliating night in the worst way.

He clicked on the flashlight in his pocket and shined it at his feet as he tiptoed up the stairs. Luckily, he made it to his bedroom without any confrontations, and after quietly closing the door behind him, he shuffled to his bed, clicked off the flashlight, and sat in the dark, feeling defeated. How could he have miscalculated Mae's feelings for him so badly, he wondered again?

Eventually, he lit the oil lantern on his nightstand and lay atop his bed, thinking about the past few months with Mae. Their relationship had grown so naturally, even though there wasn't anything seemingly natural about what happened tonight.

She led me on. The more he thought about it, his heartbreak began turning to anger. Maybe he was just filling a void in her life, helping her get through this first year without her father. He would have been happy to do that, but every mutual indication had led to a romantic relationship. It seems she wouldn't have let it get to that point if she didn't care about him. Maybe she did care for him, maybe even a lot . . . but she didn't love him, or she would have said so.

His ponderings continued as he bathed in the upstairs bathroom he shared with his siblings, then dressed for bed. He tiptoed barefoot to his bedroom, hoping not to wake up anyone since he was bathing later than normal. He scrambled to the propane heater and turned it up before he snuggled beneath the covers. Despite his continuous yawns, he couldn't turn off his mind, and every time he pictured Mae's face when he'd told her he loved her, he wanted to cry, then the bitterness returned.

IT WAS around midnight when Mae woke up suddenly. There was a crash downstairs, and as she fumbled for the flashlight on her nightstand, she slipped into her robe, then scurried down the steps toward movement she heard in the kitchen.

Mae rushed to where her mother stood trembling but stopped abruptly when she saw broken glass surrounding her mother's bare feet.

"*Mamm?*" She shined the light at her own feet. She hadn't taken the time to put on socks or slippers. She was inches away from the broken glass pitcher her mother kept by her bed, made obvious by the large, cracked handle among the tinier shards. "Are you hurt?"

"*Nee*, I'm so sorry I woke you." Her mother's eyes were glazed, her face cast in a dull pallor as her bottom lip trembled. "I came to get more water, and I dropped the pitcher."

At that moment, her mother looked and spoke like a child who was frightened and in trouble.

"Don't move." Mae pushed her palm toward her mother to drive the point home. She edged her way to the kitchen door that led outside and slipped into her mother's rubber boots before grabbing the broom and dustpan.

"Glass crunched beneath the rubber soles as she grew closer to where her mother was standing. "Here." She handed her mother the flashlight and wondered why her mother hadn't used a flashlight to get to the kitchen. Maybe because it was a straight shot from her downstairs bedroom, through the den, and into the kitchen.

As her mother stood shaking, Mae swept the glass into the dustpan and dumped it in the trashcan. "Don't move," she said again, and her mother groggily nodded.

Mae went into the den and retrieved another pair of her mother's shoes. "Slip into these." She laid the shoes on the wooden floor in front of her mother. "It's too dark to see if I got all the glass. I'll try to be up before Lillian to double-check in the morning."

"I-I don't know what happened." Her mom shrugged, her lip still trembling. "It just slipped out of *mei* hand." She rubbed Mae's shoulders. "*Danki* for tending to the mess. I'm so sorry I woke you up," she said again as a touch of color returned to her face.

"It's okay. Since we're up, do you want me to make us some hot cocoa or—?"

"*Nee*. I should get back to bed. The sun will be up early, and I have much to do tomorrow." Her mother seemed to force a smile before she kissed Mae on the cheek.

Mae watched her as she shuffled back to her bedroom with Mae's flashlight shining at her feet. The mother she used to have would have noticed Mae's eyes were swollen and insisted they chat about what was ailing her.

As her mother's bedroom door clicked shut, Mae stood in the darkness since her mother had left with her flashlight. She finally slipped out of the heavy rubber boots, returning them to the designated area right outside the door, then she started back to the stairs, hoping she wouldn't step on a sliver of glass she might have missed.

Moonlight mixed with the glowing cinders from the fire and filled the living room with shadowy images. Mae pictured her father sitting in his favorite recliner to her left, his glasses low on his nose as he read the latest edition of *The Budget* newspaper. Then her eyes drifted to her mother's knitting basket next to the rocking chair in the corner, and she envisioned her mother quietly humming as she worked on her latest project. Her mother still knitted, but she hadn't heard the comfort of her sweet, wordless tunes since her father died.

In the still of the night, the clock on the mantel ticked, an owl hooted outside, and when she shifted her gaze to the window, moon rays reflected off the lightly falling snow. Despite the festive decorations and wrapped gifts, a tear rolled down her cheek as she looked at the couch. The look on John's face when she hadn't told him she loved him might haunt her forever. She recalled her aunt telling her that time would heal the grief about her father. Would time also heal a broken heart?

She heard her mother's quiet whimpers and doubted her aunt's words. Mae was filled with grief about her father, but her mother's heart was broken in a different way, and now Mae's was too.

Night after night, Mae heard her mother's soft cries, and she respected her privacy. But tonight, she padded her way to the downstairs bedroom and knocked. "*Mamm?*"

Silence.

"*Mamm*, are you awake?" Mae put her ear against the door but heard no reply. She turned to walk away, her heart sinking even more, then the door opened.

"I'm sorry. I took off with this." Her mother handed her the flashlight that she had pointed to the floor, lighting up Mae's toes. "You didn't step on any glass, did you?" her mom asked from where she stood in her bedroom, the door partially opened and clearly not an invitation to come inside.

Mae took the flashlight and shook her head. "*Nee*, I didn't step on glass. I-I just . . ." She shrugged. "I just wanted to see if you were okay." Did her mother hear the tremble in her voice? Would she wrap her arms around her to comfort her? Did she recognize the emotions of others the way she used to, always attuned to her loved ones' needs?

"*Ya, ya.* I'm fine." Her mother smiled, but Mae could tell it was forced. And as much as she hated to hear her mother crying night after night, she wished she would share her emotions with Mae, so that in turn, Mae could share hers. Maybe together they could lift some of each other's burdens. "Go back to bed, Mae. Morning will be here soon enough."

Mae didn't move as the door closed. Maybe her mother didn't see her trembling lip, her need to have a mom again, even at her age. Or maybe she just didn't care anymore.

HANNAH LEANED her head against the door until she heard her oldest daughter walk away. Mae was hurting, and Hannah had seen her daughter's bottom lip trembling as she blinked back tears. She had wanted nothing more than to embrace her, to tell her that their grief would get better with time. At least, that's the adage she'd heard so many times, but she wasn't strong enough for that. It took all her effort to contain her emotions in front of the girls. If she'd let Mae into her bedroom, cuddled her like she did when she was a child, kissed her on the cheek . . . Hannah would have fallen apart. That was not something an eighteen-year-old should have to witness.

She crawled back under her sheets, then snuggled into the Amish wedding quilt that had been a gift from her sister and several others in their quilting group. As she gingerly ran her hand across the intricate details, rings with all her favorite pastel colors, she closed her eyes and pictured Paul lying next to her. But when she reached over to his side of the bed, of course, he wasn't there. The bed felt huge, like the hole in her heart. Even in her grief, she needed to make a mental note to do a better job of stifling her late-night sobs. Mae might have heard her crying and triggered her daughter's emotions. In Hannan's mind, she had to believe they would all recover from the loss of their husband and father.

But when?

How long will it take?

She prayed constantly for the healing powers only God could provide. Through her relationship with Jesus, she had begged for comfort for all of them. Tonight, she said extra healing prayers for Mae and Lillian as they faced their first Christmas without their father. And she asked God to give her the strength to maintain a sense of normalcy when she was around her girls. It was exhausting to hold in her emotions until she was alone at night, but if she showed strength and resolve to get through this first holiday season as a widow, then it would hopefully carry over to her daughters, especially Mae. *Widow.* The word still sounded strange in her mind, and she wasn't sure she'd ever spoken it aloud.

Hannah drifted off the same way she did every night, with tears in her eyes and clutching Paul's pillow, aware of the emptiness in the bed . . . and in her heart.

CHAPTER 4

The weeks of December marched on for John, and he was glad he had work to keep his mind occupied most of the time. The Advent season should have been festive, but when thoughts of Mae pushed to the forefront of his mind, he had a hard time getting into the spirit of the season.

He took note of the red ribbons tied to evergreen trees here and there on the way to the Schrock's home and the way the snow blanketed everything around them, glistening in the early morning light. One of his sisters had attached a bell on the back of the buggy, and it jingled in rhythm with the horse's hooves. His heart was too heavy to embrace the anticipation such images and sounds should have brought on.

John guided the covered buggy to worship service with the eldest of his sisters, Sarah, who was a year younger than John. She'd insisted on riding with him alone, meaning she had something on her mind. His younger sisters, Rebecca and Anna—eight and twelve—traveled with their parents in a separate buggy.

Sarah cleared her throat. *Here it comes.*

"There's a rumor going around that you and Mae aren't seeing each other anymore," Sarah said before they were even on the main road that led to the Schrock's home where the service would be held today. "And I've noticed that you haven't been to her *haus* in almost two weeks,"

John briefly glared at his sister. He would have to face Mae today, and he hadn't seen her since his last trip to her house. She also hadn't visited the lumberyard since then. "It didn't work out."

Sarah was the romantic in the family, always with her head in a book about couples in love, and she had a huge crush on one of the guys who worked at the lumberyard. John assumed it was mutual based on Aaron's interactions with his sister. But John had assumed a lot lately, specifically that Mae loved him. He hoped neither Sarah nor Aaron stomped on each other's heart the way Mae had his.

Distance from her had only fueled his confusion. At the least, she owed him an explanation. Every time he pondered the situation, he was sure that she had acted equally as in love with him as he was with her. *Acted.* That's what she'd done.

"Why didn't it work out?" Sarah bounced in her seat when John flicked the reins, sped up, and hit a pothole in the road.

"She just wasn't the right woman for me." The truth was, Mae was the perfect woman for him. He was apparently the wrong guy for her though. John and Sarah mostly got along, but he wasn't going to share his humiliation with her.

"Hmm . . . I thought for sure that you would end up marrying her." She shrugged. "I don't know her all that well, but I like her. We've attended several quilting parties hosted by mutual friends, and of course, I see her every two weeks at worship." She tapped a finger to her chin. "So . . . who broke up with who?"

John worried that his love for Mae would bubble to the surface, and the only way to contain his emotions was to allow indifference to take over. "It's none of your business. Can you just let it go?" His voice was harsher than he'd intended.

Sarah scowled. "You don't have to be so mean about it."

John sighed, knowing his words were misdirected. "I'm sorry, Sarah. I just don't want to talk about it."

Sarah turned to face him with an eyebrow raised. "*Ach,* I see. She broke up with you."

John resisted the urge to speak to her unkindly by taking a deep breath. "No one really broke up with anyone. It just . . ." He searched for a truthful explanation. ". . . fizzled out, I guess." *And left a giant hole in my heart.*

Sarah was quiet. "I'm sorry," she said barely above a whisper.

John swallowed back a lump in his throat, and they were quiet the rest of the ride.

Mae had the reins as she and her mother, and Lillian traveled to worship service. She was nervous to see John after cutting off things between them so abruptly.

Her mother adjusted the battery-operated heater on the dashboard of the buggy. "I noticed John hasn't come to the *haus*," she said, as if reading Mae's mind. Long buggy rides had always prompted her mother to be more talkative than in their day-to-day interactions around the house, although today, Mae wished that wasn't the case. "And, to *mei* knowledge, you haven't visited him at the lumberyard. Did something happen between the two of you?"

Mae knew her mother would eventually ask why John wasn't courting her anymore. And apparently, she couldn't read minds after all, or she'd know why. "He just wasn't the right person for me." She held her breath. They might not be able to read minds, but parents could usually spot a lie.

Her mother peered at her as her eyebrows narrowed. "I'm surprised to hear that. I thought you might be in *lieb* with him."

If Mae let this conversation go on much longer, she'd be a blubbering mess by the time they arrived at worship service. She shrugged. "*Nee.*"

"Hmm . . ." her mother responded as she refocused on the road in front of them.

Mae's stomach churned with nervous anxiety about seeing John. She prayed her mother would drop the subject.

Lillian sneezed from where she was seated in the backseat. "Tissue! I need a tissue, please."

Their mother began rummaging through her purse until she found a travel pack of Kleenex, quickly handing it over her shoulder to Lillian. After blowing her nose, Lillian said she was cold. The battery-operated heater was on as high as it would go, and they all had heavy blankets wrapped around them. Mae was warm in the covered buggy.

Her mother twisted around and put a hand to Lillian's head. "I think you might have a little fever."

"Then let's skip church." Lillian slapped her hands to her knees. "I'm sick."

Mae felt an adrenaline rush of hope surge through her, followed by a wave of guilt. She usually enjoyed the service, but today, she'd be relieved to miss it. Lillian whined every other Sunday about going to church, but at seven years old, three hours was a long time to sit still.

"Let's just see how you do. If you start feeling bad, we can leave early." Her mother handed Mae's younger sister the travel pack of Kleenex. "Keep these in the pocket of your apron in case you need one."

Lillian did as she was told, and Mae's body tensed when the Schrock's house came into view. It was a smaller crowd than usual, but sometimes the older folks couldn't get out in the weather when it was this cold and snowing, as was the case with both sets of Mae's grandparents. Mae had hoped it would be a full house, easier to stay out of view and away from John.

After Mae tethered the horse to the fencepost, she scurried to catch up to her mother and Lillian, then rushed across the threshold as they began shedding their heavy coats, black bonnets, and snow boots. After Mae placed her boots atop the pile and found space on the long rack by the door for her coat and bonnet, she padded toward the kitchen in her socks, prepared to help with the meal that would be served after worship service. Her mother was by her side. Lillian ran off to find children her age. She didn't look sick to Mae, and Mae didn't want her sister to feel bad, but she didn't want to stay for the entire service, especially the meal when everyone would be wandering and socializing.

The kitchen was full of women shuffling around in their socks, but Mae and her mother left the room when Nellie Schrock said they had everything under control.

Mae spotted John across the room talking with a woman about Mae's age—the beautiful and highly sought-after Bethany Troyer. Her stomach lurched as she stopped in her tracks and stared at them. Her mother kept going and fell into a conversation with Aunt Ruth. Mae remained frozen and unable to look away from John and Bethany, especially when Bethany laughed, put her hand on John's arm, and flashed her pearly white teeth at him. Bethany had huge green eyes and beautiful blonde hair that would often escape in ringlets from her prayer cap. Mae had always wondered why John had never courted Bethany the way everyone else in their district had done. No one had snagged her yet. Maybe she'd been waiting for John to pursue her.

As the knot in her throat grew larger, she blinked back tears. She couldn't have meant much to John if he'd already moved on to someone else. Her tears turned to anger almost right away when John whispered something in Bethany's ear before he touched her arm and walked away. Bethany smiled, then John looked right at Mae and locked eyes with her for a couple of seconds before walking in the opposite direction from where she was standing.

Jealousy was a sin, but it wrapped around Mae like a serpent, squeezing the life out of her as her stomach roiled and her heart burned with a betrayal she wasn't justified to have. Mae was the one who hadn't responded to John's admission that he loved her. She was the one who hadn't visited him at the lumberyard or invited him to her house. Their relationship's demise was her fault, and that's what she wanted.

Or so she thought.

Why was her heart putting up such a fight?

This wasn't the time or place to try to make sense of that battle. Instead, she needed to stay strong and make it through the service. Resolving, then, to listen to her head and not her heart, she pursed her lips and gritted her teeth so hard she had to be careful not to crack a tooth.

IT WAS easy for John to avoid Mae during the worship service since the men sat on one side facing the women in the Schrock's den with the bishop and elders in the middle of the room. He tried not to look at her, but occasionally he couldn't help himself and glanced at her. Not once did he catch her looking in his direction. But he had captured her glare when he'd talked to Bethany earlier. He had seen Mae enter the room, and John intentionally flirted with Bethany, even though he hadn't ever been interested in her. She was pretty, and lots of guys his age ogled her and tried to date her, but she wasn't John's type. Even though she was beautiful, she was too giggly, gossiped a lot, and only one woman held his heart.

John knew what Mae's anger looked like. He'd only seen it once while they were in town eating a burger. Mae had looked out the window by their booth just in time to see a man kick a stray dog. She jumped from her seat holding her plate before John could stop her. She scurried outside and yelled at the man, who only shrugged before he walked away, then Mae gave the starving animal the rest of her burger after removing the onions and ultimately found the dog a good home.

The only other time he'd seen her face turn that red and her eyes blaze with anger was before the service when he'd caught her looking at him flirting with Bethany. He should have felt good about it, that she was jealous. A part of him wanted to hurt her the way she'd hurt him. But he couldn't make another person love him. He reminded himself that she'd played the part well, though, and had led him on.

When the service was over, John realized he had spent most of his time analyzing what had happened between him and Mae, and he'd missed most of what the bishop talked about. He would need to ask forgiveness during devotions this evening, for allowing himself to be distracted. But even as the congregation stood and people began to mingle, John's eyes roamed the room in search of Mae.

Where is she?

Had she sprinted ahead of the other women to get to the kitchen and help prepare the meal?

It wasn't until after most of the women were in the kitchen that he saw her standing alone by herself near the hallway entrance. He waited to see if she was going down the hall to the bathroom, but she didn't move, and she had a hand across her stomach. When her lips began to tremble, John's heart pounded in his chest as he spontaneously moved toward her. He couldn't get to her fast enough. She might not love him, but even distance couldn't keep him from loving her. And something was wrong.

CHAPTER 5

*M*ae's feet were rooted to the floor even though she wanted to run away. She'd allowed her emotions to take over as if her feelings were a runaway train she couldn't control. No matter the circumstances and her fears about commitment, she'd had three hours to think about a life without John, barely hearing most of what the bishop said. It had been ample time for her moods to flip-flop between anger about Bethany . . . and regret. She'd ultimately ended up feeling more regret than anger.

As John approached her, she held her breath. In the distance, she could see her mother watching her, with eyebrows drawn and eyes questioning.

"Are you okay?" John tilted his head slightly as his eyes reflected sincere concern.

"I-I . . ." Mae didn't think she could speak without crying. Standing in the middle of the room, she could feel more people looking at them amid the quiet chatter. A few folks had already moved out to the barn where

34

heaters warmed the space they would soon use to share a meal. "Sorry." She lowered her head. It was all she could manage to say, and it was how she felt. Elaborating would only make things worse.

"Can we go somewhere and talk?" John gazed into her eyes the familiar way she'd only seen in her dreams lately, and she wanted nothing more than to throw her arms around him and tell him how much she loved him.

"I can't." She wanted to keep her head down, but she eventually raised her eyes to his. "I mean, I'm expected to help with the meal."

"Then can we talk after the meal?" John's eyes pleaded with her, and they couldn't go on like this forever. She would tell him that she cared about him very much, that she was sorry that she had let things go on for as long as she had, and apologize for leading him on.

"Okay." She wasn't sure she'd be able to eat anything, but it would give her time to organize her thoughts.

She slowly edged around him when her mother motioned for her to come her way. Lillian was at her side now.

"I'm sorry to do this because I saw you talking with John, but Lillian is for sure running a fever." Her mother was holding her little sister's hand. "I think we need to go. I'll find us something to eat at home."

"Mae-Mae, I don't feel *gut*." Lillian tugged on Mae's dress with her free hand.

Saved. Mae hated that her sister was sick, but for today, she would be able to avoid a more detailed conversation with John.

"It's okay, Lillian. Really." She felt her sister's forehead. "*Ya*, she's pretty warm."

"I already told Nellie that we were going to sneak out. She gave me some children's Tylenol for Lillian, but she understood that I wanted to get her home and tucked into bed." She motioned for Mae to follow her toward the front door where they stopped and bundled up like everyone else was doing before heading to the barn. "I should have told your Aunt Ruth, but I couldn't find her or your uncle."

Mae untethered the horse, then got the heater going while her mother covered up Lillian with an extra blanket in the backseat.

She backed up the buggy and got on the road without looking toward the crowd in the barn, afraid she would see John through one of the two opened doors, which might cause her to cry. She wasn't doing that.

Mae's mother waited until Lillian had dozed off in the backseat before she said anything. "I saw you talking to John. Did that go well?"

Her mother was a professional at hiding her emotions. Mae would have to learn from her. Might as well practice now. She cleared her throat, blowing a breath of cold air in front of her. "We didn't have time to say much. But it's fine. It doesn't matter."

"Um . . ." Her mother snuggled into the blanket she had around her. "By the look on both of your faces, it appeared to matter."

Mae fought the urge to lash out at her mother. Suddenly, she was present and available. Where had she been since their father died? "*Mamm* . . ." She took a deep breath, reminding herself of the endless nights her mother cried herself to sleep. Mae didn't have the heart to add to her suffering. *"Mamm,"* she said in a gentler voice. "John told me he *liebed* me."

For the first time since her father died, her mother smiled a real and genuine smile as she pressed her palms together and closed her eyes. "How wonderful." She opened her eyes and turned to Mae. "Falling in *lieb* is a wonderful thing."

Mae wanted to say—*Is it? Because it will destroy you if that person dies.* Instead, she said, *"Mamm,* I already told you that John is not the man for me. I don't *lieb* him." Saying the lie aloud caused her chest to tighten.

Her mother's expression fell. "Are you sure? Because all the time when he was at the *haus,* all your visits to—"

"Ya, I'm sure. I don't *lieb* him and dragging it out would have only made things worse." She hated lying to her mother, but even more so, she disliked robbing her mother of the real contentment she seemed to feel at the thought of Mae and John being in love. And she still hadn't explained anything to John. Deep down, she knew he deserved an explanation, but she was glad it wasn't happening today.

They were quiet the rest of the way home.

JOHN COULDN'T BELIEVE Mae had left with her mother and sister before the meal. Had she purposefully avoided talking to him by convincing her family to leave early? Frustration roared in his hungry stomach, but his appetite had left him when he saw Mae pull away in the buggy.

He picked at his food out in the barn, but as soon as he was done, he made his way to the kitchen where he found Mae's aunt. "Ruth, can I talk to you for a minute?"

She wiped her hands on a kitchen towel, then followed John to the mud room. "Why did your sister leave with Mae and Lillian before the meal? Is everything okay?" He tried to keep the desperation he felt out of his question.

Ruth shrugged. "As far as I know, everything is all right." She scratched her cheek. "It's unlike them, though, to leave without saying anything, especially before they even ate. I'll call Hannah from *mei* cell phone when I get home. I forgot to bring it."

John had never wanted a cell phone more than he did right now. The bishop allowed cell phones for emergencies and business use. John's parents didn't approve of the devices, and said it was an abused privilege. Technically, John could have bucked up to his folks since he was in his *rumschpringe*, but while he was under their roof, he mostly respected their rules—at least the ones they felt strongly about such as the use of mobile phones.

"I'm sure everything is fine." Ruth tapped him on the arm before giving him an all-knowing half-smile. Surely, Mae's aunt was aware that he and Mae hadn't spent any time together recently. He wanted to broach the subject, but it felt awkward, and she was gone before he had the chance to come up with a question that didn't sound desperate.

Luckily Sarah was ready to go home shortly after the meal, and he was grateful that she didn't ask him any more questions about Mae. John's mind was already on overdrive. He supposed he could go to Mae's house to make sure everyone was all right, but she'd been so hesitant to even talk to him, that he was nervous to approach her again. He was just going to have to accept that it was over. It had been a wonderful three months, but if he ever fell in love again—which he doubted—he would proceed with a lot more caution.

MAE PREPARED CHICKEN soup and turkey sandwiches while her mother tended to Lillian, whose fever still hadn't broken.

"She's tucked into bed," her mother said as she walked into the kitchen. "I'll take her some soup if she doesn't feel like coming downstairs soon."

"I hope she doesn't have the flu." Mae stirred the soup atop the stove. "Christmas is only a week away."

Her mother sat at the kitchen table. "I hope not too."

She looked over her shoulder just in time to see her mom yawning. "*Mamm*, why don't you go take a nap. I can check on Lillian and take her some soup."

"*Nee*." Her mother grinned, which was nice to see. "I'm hungry, and somehow your chicken soup is always better than mine, which is odd since I taught you to make it, and it's *mei* recipe."

That was twice that Mae had seen her mother smile today. Real smiles, not the kind she put on for show. Mae would have felt more hopeful about her mom's grief getting a little better if she didn't feel so miserable herself.

She missed her father terribly, but whatever this heartbreak was that she was feeling for John was different. She couldn't control what happened to her father, but she could control her own love life. And under different circumstances, she'd be crying on her mother's shoulder. She would stay hopeful that her mother was slowly returning to her and Lillian, but she wasn't going to add her burdens to her mother's overwhelming grief.

"Here you go." She placed a bowl of soup in front of her mother, along with half of a turkey sandwich, prepared the way she liked with just turkey, mustard, and pickles. "And I'm sure the soup doesn't taste better than yours."

Her mother blew on a spoonful before tasting the soup. "*Ya*, it's better than mine. You're putting some secret ingredient in it." She pointed the spoon at her and giggled." It was like a beautiful melody, her laughter, and it soothed Mae's soul.

Something was changing. Mae wasn't sure why her mother's attitude had shifted, but it made the sting about John lessen, if only a little. She was careful not to think about him too much and would take that cue from her mother and wait until she was alone to let her emotions spill out. And she was sure she would tonight.

CHAPTER 6

or three nights in a row, Hannah heard Mae crying. Lillian had gotten over whatever bug had latched onto her, but Hannah had been checking on her nightly. Otherwise, she might not have known how upset her oldest daughter was. And she didn't know if it was grief about her father or about not seeing John, or a combination of it all. But Mae had always talked to her about things, and Hannah suspected that she hadn't been truthful about the end of her relationship with John.

Hannah had made it a point to be more cheerful during the day and to mute her own misery at night, sometimes successfully, and other times she still cried herself to sleep. But worrying about Mae took priority over her own grief right now.

Tonight, she knocked softly on Mae's door. "Mae, are you okay? Can I come in?"

She heard her daughter sniffle. "*Mamm*, I just want to be alone. Is that okay?"

Hannah's eyes filled with tears, but this time it was for

her daughter, and not all she had lost. She opened her mouth to tell Mae that it wasn't okay and that she was coming in, but she reminded herself of all the times Mae had knocked on her door and asked if she was all right, asked if she could come in, and Hannah always said she wanted to be alone. For now, she would respect that. "Okay," she said softly. "But I'm here if you need me."

No answer.

Hannah hadn't been there as much as she could have been for her children. Their basic needs had been met, but she had emotionally checked out at certain times. Her girls deserved parental support now more than ever, especially with their first Christmas season minus Paul approaching, so she was going to work on being a better mother.

As she climbed back into bed, she reached her arm across the empty space where Paul used to sleep, but her grief over her husband wasn't shredding her insides as much as the thought of her daughter crying upstairs. Even though Hannah had been emotionally absent, it had seemed kinder than to cry in front of her children. Today, she had tried to be more emotionally attuned to her children, but still, her oldest daughter cried upstairs. She threw back the covers, sat up, and eased into her slippers, prepared to go upstairs and pull Mae into her arms. But, again, she thought of all the times Mae had tried to comfort her, and she had wanted to just be left alone. Sighing, she fluffed her pillows and laid down again. Tomorrow was Christmas Eve. She would try to be festive and make it a good day for Mae and Lillian.

MAE PULLED her knees to her chest and snuggled into her down comforter as tears wet her pillow. It took everything she had not to run downstairs, crawl into bed with her mother, and let her mother stroke her hair the soothing way she did when Mae was a child. But Mae wasn't a child anymore. She was a grown woman . . . or maybe an almost-grown woman at eighteen.

As she faced her first Christmas without her father, she wondered what the next few days would be like. A normal Christmas Eve consisted of cooking all day long, her mother humming, Lillian shaking presents that were scattered throughout the house . . . and her father being particularly flirty with her mother. Her parents had always been affectionate, but something about Christmas seemed to bring out the best in all of them, and her father had been no exception.

Her parents loved each other deeply. Mae had always known that as far back as she could remember. If they quarreled—and Mae was sure they must have—it was never in front of her or Lillian. They had kissed a lot, and her mother would blush and playfully say, "Paul, not in front of the *kinner*."

Mae longed for that kind of love with John, but it just wasn't worth taking a chance that something would happen to him. Memories of her father and Christmases past floated through her mind like a fog that might never lift, and within the denseness of her recollections, thoughts of John were lightning bolts within her storm of emotions. But she held her breath for a few seconds when she heard a noise in her sister's bedroom. It sounded like crying, and Mae moved quickly to get to her.

Mae didn't knock but flung open Lillian's door and within the shadows of darkness, she saw her sister sitting up in bed rubbing her eyes and choking back sobs.

She went to the bed, sat, and pulled Lillian into her arms. "Are you feeling sick?"

Her sister shook her head. "*Nee*. I miss *Daed*." Lillian cried harder.

Mae held her tighter. "I know you do, sweetheart." She stroked her sister's long brown hair, and again she recalled the way her mother used to do the same thing when Mae was hurting. Mae wondered how many times Lillian had cried herself to sleep. Mae had done so plenty of times since her father's death, but both she and Lillian functioned with a level of normality her mother didn't seem to have anymore . . . even though Mae had seen the rebirth of her mother a little today.

"Will you read me a story?" Lillian's voice cracked as she spoke, her tears spilling out against Mae's nightgown.

She eased her sister away, pushed loose strands of hair from her tiny face, then said, "*Nee*, I won't. But I have a better idea." She rummaged around on the nightstand until she found her sister's flashlight and clicked it on. She stood, lifted Lillian into her arms, gave her a tight squeeze, then set her down. Lillian wore thick socks to bed. Mae wished she'd taken the time to slide into her slippers as the cold floor sent a chill the length of her body. But she held Lillian's hand, and together they went downstairs, the smells of the season wafting up their nostrils as they neared the first floor. Cinnamon comingled with pine, and in the near darkness with only the flashlight on, Mae took in the colorful wrapped presents and decorations, and how it all represented the anticipatory feel of Christmases past.

Mae was almost dragging Lillian across the living room, then hesitated at her mother's bedroom door, listening . . . to her crying. But she didn't knock. She pushed the door open. "*Mamm*."

Her mother sprung to a sitting position, and Mae was able to make out her actions in the dark as she struggled to wipe away tears before she flipped on the flashlight she kept on her nightstand. She shined it right at Mae and Lillian, then gasped.

"*Mei maeds*, what's the matter? Why are you both crying?"

"We miss *Daed*," Lillian said through her tears. She broke away from Mae and ran to her mother's open arms.

"I know you do, *mei* sweet girl." As her mother welcomed Lillian in her arms, gently rocking back and forth, stroking her hair, Mae stood in the doorway with tears rolling down her cheeks. She didn't need an invitation to join them, but she wanted one, and she didn't have to wait long. Her mother motioned for Mae to come in, and when she got into bed, her mother held them both, and together they all cried as if their father had died that very day, not six months ago. Their mother sobbed the hardest.

"I *lieb* you *maeds* so much," she said, her voice shaking with emotion. "I know you're hurting, but we will get through this first Christmas without your beloved *daed* as best we can."

"Together," Mae said softly as her mother stroked her hair in the same soul-soothing way she was doing with Lillian.

"*Ya*, together." Her mother pulled them both closer.

For the first time since the death of her husband, Mae and Lillian's mother wept openly, and showed true emotion, and even though sadness filled the room, there was also relief. Mae realized that now they could face Christmas together, not alone in solitude, faking emotions, and pretending everything was okay. As she embraced this new reality, a calmness began to settle over her, and she realized for the first time the true love of family that her father continued to gift them . . . even in his absence.

JOHN WAS LATE FOR BREAKFAST, which was a big no-no on Christmas Eve morning, and it would have been even worse if it had been Christmas Day. He would need to set the alarm on his battery-operated clock for tomorrow morning.

"Sorry," he said as he glanced around the table at his three sisters and parents.

After they prayed silently, everyone dug into the first of several special meals his mother and sisters prepared for Christmas Eve and Christmas Day. The day after Christmas would be equally as festive. On Second Christmas they would visit shut-ins and continue to cele-brate the birth of Jesus. To his knowledge, Second Christmas wasn't celebrated by the English. John usually considered the extended holiday as one of the perks of being Amish. This year, he just wanted to get through the holidays and be done with it.

John eyed the loaf of cinnamon bread, pan of blueberry muffins, a potato and egg casserole, the platter of sausage and bacon, stack of pancakes, bowl of fresh fruit, and bowl of scrambled eggs. "Something for everyone," his mother always said on special occasions. John wasn't sure he could eat any of it, even though his stomach grumbled in resistance. He'd dreamed about Mae in between tossing and turning all night thinking about her. He also wondered what he would do with the Christmas present he'd made for her before he found out she didn't love him, and apparently didn't even want to talk to him.

He did his best to eat a little of the meal his sisters and mother had prepared, but after breakfast and the clean-up, his oldest sister found him out in the barn, the place he went when he wanted to be alone.

Sarah crossed over the threshold, pulling her black cape snug as she sloshed into the barn, bringing snow and ice with her. Once inside, she untied her black bonnet and shook it dry. "John, it's freezing out here, but I knew this is where you would be, assuming no one would come out here looking for you." She slapped her hands to her hips. "I know you want to be alone, but you need to at least fake some sort of festiveness for Rebecca and Anna's sake. You're so transparent, and we all know you're upset about things not working out with Mae, but you are robbing everyone else of the Christmas spirit." She paused. "Please try to remember the reason for the season."

John opened his mouth to tell Sarah to go away, but

the barn door slammed shut from the wind, putting his words on pause. It was loud and jarring, and maybe a wake-up call to John. His sister was right. He chose a different approach. "I'll do *mei* best to act cheerful in front of everyone."

She walked closer to him, and with each step, her expression grew more sympathetic. "Maybe don't just *act*." She put a hand on her chest, atop her black cape as she shivered. "Let the Holy Spirit into your heart, you might be surprised at the miracles *Gott* is capable of, including the mending of a broken heart."

Sarah leaned into him and embraced him tightly. "I *lieb* you." Then she turned and left.

"I *lieb* you too," he said barely above a whisper, glad she was out of sight before his eyes became moist.

Seconds later, he dropped to his knees, clasped his hands, and took in his surroundings, reminding him of Jesus's birth in a barn and of all the suffering the Lord's son would go through to make a place for him in Heaven.

Then he prayed that he would find the Christmas spirit . . . for real.

Even without Mae.

CHAPTER 7

$\mathcal{I}$t was late afternoon on Christmas Eve when Ruth and Henry left the Kings' house, along with Hannah's parents. Paul's parents had stopped by briefly, but they hadn't stayed long since they had several other rounds of visitation scheduled with Paul's other siblings. After waving bye to the last of their guests, Hannah closed the door, turned around, and faced her children. "I think we did pretty *gut* today."

Lillian nodded. Her youngest daughter had fought tears on and off throughout the day, and tomorrow—Christmas Day—would be even harder. Hannah had managed to keep her emotions tucked away, in front of her houseguests but also so she wouldn't upset Ruth and Henry, or the atmosphere in general. She did her best to be festive even though she missed Paul more than ever.

Mae seemed to have the hardest time throughout the day, disappearing for long periods at a time, then returning with swollen eyes or a red face that looked previously streaked with tears. Hannah had hoped that by spilling their emotions the night before that maybe they'd released some of the grief they felt, grief that Hannah had been hiding from her girls. As she reflected on the past six months, maybe she'd done them more harm than good by not showing her feelings. She wasn't sure if there was a right or wrong way to behave in this situation. But Mae seemed to have stepped into Hannah's shoes by trying to corral her emotions today.

Hannah wasn't sure she wouldn't have another meltdown alone this evening, but prior to that, she was going to wait until Lillian was in bed, then try to talk to Mae.

Her oldest daughter remained quiet the rest of the day. But Lillian had spurts of little girl Christmas excitement, then she would recall something about her father, and her light dimmed. Hopefully, the special gifts Hannah had made for the girls—more than usual—would bring moments of joy.

"Mae, can we talk?" Hannah posed the question after Lillian was tucked in bed upstairs.

"Um . . ." Mae was perched on the couch with her legs tucked beneath her. She lowered her legs to the floor and closed the book she was reading. "I-I was just getting ready to bathe, and—"

"Please." Hannah bit her bottom lip, willing it not to tremble. "It won't take long."

"Okay," Mae responded with little enthusiasm, almost as if she was being punished, putting her book down before crossing her arms across her chest, then sighing. "What do you want to talk about?"

Hannah wanted to tread softly, but the subject matter wasn't going to allow it. She cleared her throat. "Since your *daed* died, I wake up in the middle of the night sometimes, and I would go upstairs and check on you and Lillian. I always find you are sleeping soundly. And I know that everyone has their own way of dealing with grief, but I don't want you to feel like you must hide it. I know you've been crying a lot today."

Her daughter's mouth fell open as her eyebrows narrowed in what appeared to be anger, which was the last thing Hannah expected. "*Mamm*, prior to last night, when I burst through your bedroom door, you've been hiding your grief from everyone. You walk around like a robot just going through the motions." She held up a hand when Hannah opened her mouth to speak up. "Before you say anything, I don't mean to sound cruel, but you've been absent since *Daed* died. Lillian and I both needed that release last night, to be comforted by our *mudder* even if it was long overdue. So, if I choose not to show *mei* grief openly, I think you should respect *mei* feelings."

Hannah's heart was cracking as she blinked back tears and took a seat next to her daughter on the couch. "Mae, I'm sorry. I thought I was doing the right thing by not breaking down constantly in front of you and your sister." She lowered her head in shame. "I should have been there more for you both." Then she couldn't hold back, and she covered her face with her hands and sobbed.

"*Mamm*, please don't cry." Mae wrapped her arms around her mother. "I'm sorry. I'm sorry I said anything. I know your loss is so much worse than mine and Lillian's." Mae was crying now, but Hannah's chest tightened as she eased her daughter away.

"What? I never claimed that *mei* loss was any worse

than yours and Lillian's. I know that you were shocked when he passed, that grief has plagued us all . . ." She swallowed back the growing lump in her throat as she sniffled. "We all suffered, and continue to suffer, equally. But it was *mei* mistake to pretend like everything was okay. I'm sorry. And knowing this, I wish I could go back six months because I would have done things differently."

"*Mamm*, you had *Daed* for a lot longer than Lillian and I did." She put her hand over her heart. "And you were so in *lieb*. Not everyone has what you and *Daed* had. I have plenty of friends who noticed over the years how happy you two were, often commenting that they wished their parents were like you and *Daed*." She shook her head. "I always used to want what you and Daed had."

Ding, ding. "What do you mean 'used to want'?" Had Hannah wrecked her daughter's life and caused her to think this way?

Mae's expression went blank as she locked eyes with Hannah. "I don't ever want to go through what you're going through." She began to cry. "To *lieb* someone so much that your heart flutters every time you're near that person, like you're floating on air, that you want to spend the rest of your life walking a foot off the ground with that person because you're so in *lieb*. I'd rather not ever *lieb* someone that way then take a chance on losing him." She lowered her head and covered her face.

Hannah's jaw had dropped somewhere along the line, so she forced her mouth closed and bit her bottom lip again. "I think it's too late, *mei lieb*. You're in *lieb* with John, aren't you?"

Mae cried harder. "*Ya*, and that's why I broke up with

him. I never meant for things to get as serious as they did, and I surely didn't mean to fall in *lieb* with him. I *lieb* him so much it physically hurts sometimes." She locked eyes with Hannah again. "There are no guarantees in life, as you well know, and *Mamm* . . . I don't want to end up like you. I miss *Daed* every day, but I know you are feeling a different kind of grief. I only feel a tiny fraction of that, and I've only been seeing John for three months. What if I had married him, then lost him the way you lost *Daed*?" She lowered her head. "I couldn't survive it. That kind of loss would kill me."

"Sometimes, it feels like it did," Hannah mumbled, wishing she hadn't said what she was thinking. "Mae, you need to understand something. I would not change one thing about *mei* life. If I could have seen the future and known your father would be killed at a young age in a terrible accident, I still would have married him." Hannah gently cupped her daughter's chin and lifted her eyes to hers. "I want you to listen to me, listen carefully. There's a popular quote . . . Is it better to have *liebed* and lost or to have never *liebed* at all? I am telling you that it is better to have *liebed* and lost than to have never shared the experience. I will miss your father for the rest of *mei* life, and I will get better over time. I know this. And as time goes by, I'll be able to find joy in our memories. I'll be able to talk about him, to recall the beautiful times we had together, and laugh at recollections of his silly jokes and behavior." She offered her daughter a weak smile. "I'm just not there yet." She cupped Mae's cheek. "Please don't give up on *lieb* for fear of losing that person. We can't know the plans *Gott* has for us, but He will never forsake us. And I know that now even amid my pain and grief." She lowered her hand to her lap, then reached for Mae's hand and squeezed it tightly between both of hers. "Don't you let John get away if you believe him to be the man of your dreams, the person you want to be with."

"I know we're young, but it feels that way, *Mamm*. Between missing him and missing *Daed* . . ." A tear slipped down Mae's cheek as she lifted her shoulders and slowly dropped them.

Hannah's heart was breaking, but it was cracking for another reason other than the death of her husband.

She squeezed Mae's hand again. "You said John told you he *liebs* you."

"*Ya*, he did." she was quick to respond.

Hannah put her hands to her face for a few seconds, taking deep breaths before she gazed at her daughter's tear-streaked face. "You're right. You're young. But so were your father and I I knew I *liebed* your *daed* two weeks after he began courting me." She nudged Mae's shoulder with hers and winked at her. "And you know what? I told him that I *liebed* him first, after only two weeks." She chuckled. "I wish you could have seen the look on his face."

Mae cocked her head to one side as she considers what her mother is saying. "Did he say it back?'

Hannah smiled. "*Ya*, he sure did. I felt like the luckiest young woman on the planet. I understand about walking on air, and God blessed us with a special relationship that maybe everyone doesn't have. And I'll take that over not ever having been with him, for sure." She paused. "Your father is not coming back to us. We must deal with that in our own ways. I apparently failed miserably as a mother with the way I handled it, and—"

"*Nee, Mamm.* Don't say that. You were doing what you thought best for your *kinner*. I shouldn't have said anything."

"I am thanking *Gott* that you did say something. Otherwise, you might have missed out on the *lieb* of your life."

"I didn't tell him I *liebed* him. I didn't even give him an explanation. He probably hates me by now." Mae swiped at her eyes when tears began to spill again.

"If that is the case, then he's not the right young man for you. But I seriously doubt he hates you. He might be confused or bitter because he doesn't understand why you just cut him off. He probably thinks you don't *lieb* him."

Mae shook her head. "And that is not true. I *lieb* him with all *mei* heart, but I just don't want to—"

"I know . . . end up like me." Hannah wished she could back up at least a few months, but she was going to need to make up for some lost time, and let the healing begin. She patted her daughter on the leg. "Wait here. I have something special I want to show you, that no one has ever seen besides your father."

Mae's eyebrows lifted and she almost had a smile on her face. Maybe Christmas could be salvaged after all. And maybe Hannah could convince her daughter that true love is worth the risk of a broken heart.

CHAPTER 8

*M*ae glanced around at the gifts stacked in various places throughout the living room. Her family had exchanged presents with her aunt and uncle and grandparents, but much to Lillian's frustration, the three of them wouldn't open their gifts to each other until tomorrow after worship service. At the time when Lillian cried about it, Mae thought her mother should have made an exception to the holiday rule, but maybe keeping traditions was a better idea.

Today, they'd had ham Aunt Ruth brought, and Mae and her mother had made potato salad, baked beans, and several other side dishes that were their own established traditions—candied carrots, creamed corn, and shaved Brussels sprout with cranberries and nuts. Her grandparents brought a salted caramel pie, an apple pie, and chocolate-peppermint brownies. In keeping with tradition, Mae's mother was slow cooking a turkey overnight, and the aroma hung in the air, in a place where memories and grief collided. Mae wondered when happiness and grief would meet in the middle and become normality.

Her mother returned to the living room with a wooden box underneath her arm about the size of a shoebox. She stopped to stoke the fire, sending orange embers wafting upward, and Mae could see a gentle snow falling outside beneath the gas lamp that lit part of the front yard, which was visible from the window behind the couch.

"What's in the box?" Mae asked her mother as she sat down. She gingerly ran her hand atop the wooden surface and smiled as she turned to Mae, whose stomach twisted with anticipation.

"*Mei* memories," her mother said softly, still running her fingers along the top of the box, which Mae noticed had her parents initials carved into the wood. "I haven't opened it since your *daed* died." She swiped at a tear.

"*Mamm*, we don't have to do this. If you don't want to show me what—"

"*Ya, ya*. I do. I want you to know that every moment I spent with your father was worth the grief I am feeling now." She gently cupped Mae's cheeks and locked eyes with her before she lowered her hands and unhooked the latch.

Mae gasped when she saw some of the contents on top. "Pictures? They're not allowed." All Amish knew that. Taking photographs violated the Second Commandment that prohibited making graven images.

Her eyes widened when her mother picked up a handful of photographs. There were other things in the box, but Mae was transfixed on the top picture her mother showed her.

"We had a *rumschpringe*, you know." She chuckled. "And we didn't let it go to waste."

"Wow," Mae said softly as her mother handed her the photo. "You were so young." She laughed. "And look at those blue jeans and T-shirts." She'd never seen her parents dressed in anything besides traditional Amish attire.

"We were younger than you. Both of us were seventeen." Her mother leaned closer to Mae and rested her head on her shoulder. "He was the most handsome, wonderful, loving boy—who was almost a man—I'd ever met."

"*Ya*, *Daed* was handsome, for sure." She pulled the photo closer. "Aw, you're holding hands. Where was this taken?" Mae could see the corner of a house and a pond in the background. It looked familiar, but she couldn't place it in her mind.

"We were behind The Peony Inn." Everything, including Mae's heart, felt lighter when her mother laughed. "You know that Esther and Lizzie, the owners, are known matchmakers. And they were back then too. Lizzie took that picture. "Paul—your *daed*—*liebed* to fish, and once when I was visiting the widows, they asked me to take the young man down at the pond some tea. He was from another district and doing some work on the barn for Esther and Lizzie. I'd never met him before." She laughed again. "Esther took credit for introducing us. Lizzie took credit for all the times she nudged us together." She shrugged. "Their matchmaking wasn't necessary.

It was *lieb* at first sight for me. And your father told me later that it was for him too."

Her mother handed her another picture of them standing in front of a movie theater, then they flipped through several photos that were taken in restaurants. All the Amish Mae knew frequented restaurants, but she'd only known a few teenagers in their running around period who had gone to a movie. Mae secretly hoped she would be able to do so before she was baptized, and apparently, her parents had seen a movie together.

"Who took these pictures?" Mae knew lots of Amish folks who had cell phones, but she was pretty sure selfies were not popular twenty years ago.

"We had a regular old camera, the kind where you had to go have the photos developed. We would ask people to take pictures of us, and no one knew we were Amish since we were wearing *Englisch* clothes." She giggled. "Except for Lizzie when she took that picture of us at The Peony Inn, but she's always been a tad nontraditional."

"Where's this?" Mae eyed a faded photo, unable to make out the object in the picture.

"Jug Rock."

Mae pulled the picture closer to her face until the image came into focus and she recognized the only free-standing table rock formation east of the Mississippi. "In Shoals, right?"

"*Ya*. It's where we had our first kiss. No one was around to take a picture of us . . ." She laughed, which was becoming a magical melody Mae had missed so much. "Nor did we want anyone around. So, we took a picture of the rock."

"*Ach*, look at this." She pulled out a string with a tiny cross, a necklace. "We each had one, but your *daed* lost his on a rollercoaster."

Now it was Mae who roared with laughter. "I cannot even imagine you and *Daed* on a rollercoaster." She handed the picture to her mother. "Well, I haven't been putting *mei rumschpringe* to *gut* use. I need to get busy."

"We did have a lot of fun . . . but only for three months. Then we were baptized and married a month later."

Her mother set the photos and necklace aside and began going through the other items in the box, each with a story or memory attached to it. And her mother smiled the entire time, an occasional tear, but there were fond recollections, laughter, and all Mae could think was *I have* mei *mom back.*

Would it last? She didn't know. But, at this very moment, she wanted her mother to know how she felt. Aside from the wonderful smell of turkey cooking, the fire crackling, the light snowfall that continued, Mae wanted her mom to know how special this Christmas was to her, despite the void.

"*Mamm?*"

Her mother turned to her, eyes glistening, but not from tears. There was a glow about her that Mae hadn't seen in a long time. "*Ya?*"

"*Danki.* This is the best Christmas present you could have ever given me." A tear rolled down her cheek, and her mother's soft thumb was there to gently wipe it away.

"You're welcome, sweet child of mine." Her mother closed the box and hooked the latch, then held it against her chest. "There will still be tears, but *mei* memories will sustain me, and I promise to be more transparent with *mei* feelings. I want you to do the same." She smiled. "I'm glad we opened this box together."

"Me too." She threw her arms around her mom. "I *lieb* you so much."

"I *lieb* you, too, and your *daed liebed* you and Lillian very much also. He would want us to be happy." Then she eased away, pressed her lips together, and tapped Mae on the nose with her finger, grinning. "Now, don't you let that boy get away. Do you hear me?"

Mae nodded, then thanked God for the wonderful Christmas Eve she'd been blessed with.

JOHN STRUGGLED to keep his sister's advice in the forefront of his mind—*remember the reason for the season.* The service was being held at The Peony Inn, and thankfully so since the large house was roomy enough for everyone to have a place to eat indoors. It was another smaller service, though, due to the weather, John assumed.

But even the aroma of a simmering meal and the festive decorations throughout the home didn't propel his emotions in the right direction. Sitting through Christmas Day worship with a clear view of Mae and her family pulled his mind away from the service. By the time the bishop wrapped things up, John realized he'd been so preoccupied that he had stumbled his way through the prayers and scripture readings without retaining much of what was said.

His mood shifted when the service was over, and Mae asked if she could talk to him after the meal. He nodded with too much enthusiasm. After she'd walked away, he accepted the possibility that her wanting to chat with him might not have anything to do with how she felt about him. It might be something totally unrelated, but he couldn't help but feel hopeful.

Lizzie and Esther, owners of the inn, along with the other women, had prepared a lavish display. The bishop allowed things to be fancier during the holidays, and The Peony Inn glowed with Christmas spirit. White cloths covered the additional tables set up in the large dining room, all with holly wreaths around candelabras with red candles. One table was against the wall and filled with beautifully decorated desserts.

Still . . . it was the longest meal of John's life, but when Mae finally approached him, he couldn't get up fast enough. Most folks were in the dining room still eating and chatting.

"Can we talk? Maybe in the den over by the fireplace? It will be more private." Mae held up a finger. "I just need to do something quickly. Can you meet me there in about two minutes?"

"Uh, *ya*." John's mind scrambled with confusion. Mae was chipper, fueling his hope that whatever she had to say would be related to their relationship, but she'd been clear about how she felt about him.

As the fire crackled nearby, sprawling orange flames warming the space, John waited for what felt longer than two minutes. Three of the elders were in the far corner of the room, but they were in deep conversation.

"Sorry, it took longer than I thought," she said as sidled up next to him, the closest he'd been to her in a long time. He breathed in the familiar scent of her lavender shampoo and lotion. "I had to take care of something. But . . ." She lowered her head, and when she looked up, she had tears in her eyes.

"What's wrong?" His hope was chipping off like pieces of an already broken heart.

"I'm sorry for something else too." She glanced at the three men in the corner, their heads still buried in a circle of conversation, then she threw her arms around him and hung on tightly. "I *lieb* you," she whispered in his ear. "I *lieb* you with all *mei* heart."

He eased her away and locked eyes with her. "But you didn't say—"

"I know, I know. I was so scared. Terrified of losing you. We are grieving about losing *mei daed*, but I've watched *mei mudder* grieve in a way I didn't know was possible, and I *lieb* you so much that I didn't ever want to feel that way. But *mei mudder* convinced me that it is better to have *liebed* and lost than to never *lieb* at all. And if you'll still have me, I—"

"Still have you?" John didn't think he could smile any broader as he cupped her cheeks with both hands. "You are the *lieb* of *mei* life. I'm sure of it."

"And I feel the same way, John." Mae's face, illuminated by the glow of twinkling lights atop the mantle of the fireplace, shone with truth and sincerity. The warmth of the Christmas spirit finally found him as the chipped pieces of his broken heart began to mend.

He kissed her again before he eased away and said, "I

made something for you before you stopped talking to me. I almost didn't bring it, but I felt a nudge I couldn't ignore and put it in *mei* buggy at the last minute."

She lowered her gaze. "I-I'm afraid I don't have a gift for you."

He cupped her cheeks again until she finally looked up. "Your *lieb* is the best Christmas present ever. Nothing can top that." He held up one finger. "Wait here." Then he dashed out the front door of the inn without putting on his coat. Luckily it had stopped snowing, and he grabbed the gift bag he'd put in the backseat.

Breathless, he ran back to the house and met her beside the fireplace, and the warmth of the fire spread to his heart as he handed her the gift. A few more people had gathered in the living room, but the fireplace at the inn was enormous, and no one paid much attention to them off to one side of it.

Smiling, Mae removed the tissue from the bag, then gasped when she saw what was inside. "*Ach*, John."

"I carved the box." He eyed the two hearts he had whittled into the front of the cedar, barely crossing over each other.

She gingerly undid the latch and ran her hand across the white felt he'd glued inside.

"Our hearts will always be as one." Clutching the box, she leaned up on her toes and kissed him the way he remembered, filled with passion . . . and love. His heart was full. He could feel eyes on them, but he didn't care. Mae loved him, and that was all that mattered.

"Best Christmas ever," he said between kisses. "I'll remember this moment for the rest of *mei* life."

"Me too." She kissed him again just as Lizzie came flying around the corner.

Lizzie, the petite co-owner of The Peony Inn, stood in the entryway to the den with her husband looking over her shoulder and strands of gray hair flying loose from beneath her prayer covering. "I'm sorry! I'm late!" She held up a mobile phone and addressed Mae. "Am I late?"

"*Nee*, you are just in time." Then she kissed John again as Lizzie snapped several pictures.

"Mission accomplished," Lizzie's tall husband said from behind her. "Let's let these two young people be alone."

They were hardly alone. More folks had come into the den. Photos weren't allowed, and public affection was frowned upon. But out of the corner of his eye, John caught the bishop slightly smiling. He supposed it was hard not to be joyous, even if rules were broken, when love abounded.

John looked at Mae, grinning. "What was all that about?"

"I'll explain it to you someday." Mae winked.

He pulled her close, kissed her again, and thanked God for this Christmas gift. For Mae. And for the prospect of many more Christmases together.

"Merry Christmas, Mae." John gazed into her eyes, his heart full.

She smiled. "Merry Christmas to you, too, John."

EPILOGUE

*M*any years later . . .

Mae slipped into her nightgown, fluffed her pillows, then slid into bed next to her husband. "It was a wonderful, blessed Christmas," she said as lowered the light on the lantern just a little bit.

"*Ya*, it was. We sure had a houseful." John smiled. "I counted twenty-five."

"And it will be twenty-six in a couple of months." Mae smiled as she thought about their family— six children, seventeen grandchildren, and soon-to-be great-grandchild.

Then, as was tradition, she reached for the small red suitcase that John had already retrieved from the closet and put on the edge of the bed. She opened it up and took out the cedar box he'd given her that Christmas so long ago. Her mother had long since passed, but Mae had carried on her tradition. There were baby shoes, baby clothes Mae had made, silver rattles, pictures their children and grandchildren had drawn or painted, cards for special occasions, and a host of other memorabilia they'd collected throughout their lives—including a picture standing in front of a movie theater. And, of course, the photos that Lizzie had taken of them by the fireplace at The Peony Inn.

"Look at us," she said softly. "We were so young."

"And so in *lieb*." John leaned closer and gazed at the picture before he kissed her.

She had to believe her mother was smiling down on them from heaven. And her father too. Mae and John had never shown anyone the contents of their box. Maybe one day, she or her husband would be sharing it with their children and grandchildren. *Or maybe not.*

John chuckled. "There are a lot of stories represented in that box."

Mae smiled at her husband as she recalled their long lives, the adventures they'd had, especially when they'd embraced their *rumschpringe* for all it was worth before being baptized and getting married.

"We've been blessed," she said as she put the lid on the large box.

"*Ya*, we have."

Her husband put the box back in the red suitcase, closed it, then put it back in the closet for safekeeping. They would continue to add pertinent items to their memory box, but they wouldn't go through it again until next Christmas, the way they'd been doing for sixty-two years.

"Merry Christmas, Mae."

She smiled and thanked God for the life she'd been blessed with. "Merry Christmas, John."

A REQUEST

Authors depend on reviews from readers. If you enjoyed this book, would you please consider leaving a review on Amazon?

TURN THE PAGE

. . . to read a sample of *Return of the Monarchs (An Amish Romance)*.

RETURN OF THE MONARCHS - CHAPTER ONE

Thomas picked up his straw hat from the dusty gravel road for the third day in a row, shook it, then placed it back on his head.

"Hey, Amish boy!" The English man, probably around Thomas's age—eighteen—was a tall guy, a few inches taller than Thomas. He wore jeans and a white T-shirt; his blonde hair hung almost to his shoulders. As he tucked his hands in his back pockets, he said, smirking, "Don't you want to take a swing at me?" He chuckled, as did his two buddies who were dressed similarly, one being about Thomas's size, the other a bit smaller in stature. The boy doing the talking had a red scar that ran horizontally above his right eye, visible beneath the sweat beading on his forehead.

Thomas began walking along the edge of the road that led to his house. His leg didn't hurt anymore, but he still limped from the accident. He hoped he would have his buggy back soon so he could blow past these guys and leave a plume of dust in his wake. But he also had to purchase a new horse. Molly hadn't fared as well as Thomas when the car struck them over a month ago. The mare had survived, but she would never be able to pull a buggy or plow again.

"He's not going to do anything, Rob." The tallest of the three snickered. "Just like he didn't do anything the last couple of times he crossed our paths. They're passive."

Thomas picked up his pace, hoping the three Englishers would go back to doing whatever they were doing instead of standing by the road in the middle of nowhere. They were old enough to drive a car, and they didn't seem to have any purpose being there.

When two hands slammed against his back, hard enough to drop him to his knees, he trembled with rage, but stayed down for a few seconds before he stood and began to walk again. They likely wouldn't do much as he passed by the small general store on the opposite side of the road. Thomas had a sick thought. Maybe they were planning to rob Herron's General Store. There wasn't much else within a half mile or so, only the Byler's place and The Peony Inn, both tucked far off the road. Montgomery, Indiana was a small town with a sizable Amish population, and Thomas's family often did business with members of the community who weren't Amish. He wasn't sure where these three guys lived or came from, but they were more aggressive today. They'd only slung vulgarities his way the past couple of days.

Back on his feet, his right leg throbbed, the one with a pin inside near his knee.

The three guys sped up until they were in front of him, blocking his way. Thomas stopped, facing them as sweat pooled at his temples, and an inner rage boiled as hot as the searing sun. "Don't you have something better to do?"

The small guy folded his arms across his chest as the crook of his mocking smile rose on one side. "Not really. Where's your horse and buggy anyway?"

Thomas didn't want to talk about the accident. "Look, I don't want any trouble. I'm just walking home from work." He wasn't sure he would be able to control his temper if the guy hit him. He'd never been struck in the face, at least not by a fist. Once, a fence post popped loose while he was making repairs and bruised his face, but he'd never been punched.

But it was coming. The short guy stepped forward, clearly unintimidated by the fact that Thomas was taller and more muscular. Maybe all three guys were going to jump him at once. Would he fight back? Would God forgive him? Would he forgive himself?

The tallest of the trio eased his friends to the side. "Arnie, Jeff . . . step aside. I'm the same size as this punk. It needs to be a fair fight."

Thomas looped his thumbs beneath his suspenders, blinking away sweat that was getting in his eyes. "What exactly are we going to fight about? I don't even know you."

"Cuz you live like backwoods trash. Your kind steals jobs away from our families." He poked a finger on Thomas's chest, which fueled his desire to knock this guy out.

"Yeah . . . your father recently outbid Jeff's dad on a big construction job." He nodded to the middle-sized guy. "You're literally taking food off our table. Seems you should stick to working for your own people and stay away from us normal people."

The speaker appeared to be Arnie, which meant the middle guy was Jeff, but he didn't know the name of the person facing off with him. And, for some reason, it became an important detail.

"What's your name?" Thomas lifted his chin a bit higher and adjusted his expression to hide the bubble of fear rising to the surface.

The guy laughed, glancing back and forth at Arnie and Jeff. "I'm about to put my fist in this jerk's face and he wants to know my name?" He shrugged, sporting a Cheshire cat grin. "Sure. I'll tell you my name. Brian Edwards." An eyebrow above his left eye rose. "Ring any bells?"

"As in Edward's Construction?" Thomas wasn't sure why anyone in the Edwards' family would care about losing a bid to Thomas's father. They were a wealthy family by all comparisons, and if the other two were friends of the family, Thomas doubted his family was taking food off any of their tables.

"That would be correct." He nodded to Arnie and Jeff. "All three of our fathers do the construction around here." He snickered. "Well, they hire grunts to do it. They don't have to swing any hammers like I'm sure your old man does."

Thomas was proud of their family business and the way his father had worked to build it into a notable success. They weren't rich and tried to live a simple life, but Thomas worked hard alongside his father, who was still at work on the job now. Thomas left early each day to get home to feed and tend the animals. He'd never minded the mile long walk before a couple of days ago.

Based on the conversation, Thomas was starting to feel like they'd sought him out intentionally. "*Ya*, well. Get on with it then. You know I'm not going to hit you back. I'm guessing this is some sort of warning for us not to offer up any construction bids if you're bidding too."

Brian rubbed his stubbled chin. His hair was dark and parted to one side, a bit more clean-cut than Arnie and Jeff. "I admit, it's irritating when we lose a job to your father, but this is more about . . ." He lowered his head, sighed, then looked up grinning. "We just don't like your kind. I mean, it's weird. The way you live. No electricity, no cars . . ." He pointed to Thomas's black slacks, short-sleeved blue shirt held up with suspenders, then nodded to his straw hat. "And the stupid way you dress."

"You have a right to your opinion, but that doesn't give you the right to instigate a fight." Thomas was sure he wasn't going to win this debate, and he could already see his mother and two sisters fussing over him when he came home with a black eye, busted lip, broken jaw, or whatever else Edward's punch might inflict.

"Whoa—instigate—a big word for a guy who only has an eighth-grade education. Impressive."

Thomas braced himself when he saw Brian curl both fists at his side.

"Just hit him, and let's go," Arnie said. "The girls are waiting at Tina's house."

They all turned toward the general store across the street when the door slammed shut.

"Who's that? Doesn't some older lady run that store?" Jeff asked. "Who's that chick all dressed in black?"

Thomas, like the other three, watched as a girl stomped down the porch steps of the store, then march toward them. If these guys thought he dressed weird, they were going to have a field day with this girl. She had on tight black pants, black boots halfway up her calves, a long-sleeved black shirt that was tucked in and held by a silver belt adorned with tiny silver crosses. A long silver cross hung around her neck. Black tresses of hair fell below her waist, and her eyes cast a shadow on her cheeks as she grew near, her long black eyelashes touching her upper lids. She had a silver ring in her nose and three in one ear. Even her fingernails were painted black.

She stopped in front of their foursome. She couldn't have been much more than five foot tall. Short and skinny. Bright red lipstick covered her full lips. She was sort of pretty, but it was hard to tell with all the dark makeup she wore.

After she slammed her hands to her hips, she said, "Do we have a problem here?"

Something about the way she said it left them all momentarily speechless.

Brian smiled. "No. Not at all. In fact, we're on our way to a little party." He eyed her up and down in a way that left Thomas feeling sick, sizing her up like she was a meal to be devoured. "Care to join us? It's just down the road."

"Don't you have a car?" She presented a flat-lipped smile, the kind he'd seen his sisters flash when they were mad, not a real smile.

"We all have cars," Brian said. "But we wanted to stop

and talk to our friend, so we decided to walk today." He nodded to Thomas, who wasn't even sure if these guys knew his name.

She smiled the not-so-real smile again and pointed over her shoulder. "Well, that's my car, and I'm driving *my friend* home." She latched on to Thomas's hand and pulled with the strength of someone twice her size.

They were halfway to the car when she turned around. "Brian Edwards, if I catch you bullying any of the Amish around here again, I'll have my father get in touch with yours. Although, I halfway expect he's as big a bully as you." She pointed her finger at each one of them. "As all of you."

Thomas attempted to shake loose of her hand, but he didn't try very hard. She had a firm hold on him, and he'd never held an English girl's hand.

Brian laughed loudly before he shouted back at her. "Coming from someone who dresses like you? Oooh, I'm scared. Shaking in my boots." He held up his hands. "But we'll get on down the road. We have some hot *normal* girls waiting for us."

After Brian, Jeff, and Arnie started walking, the girl abruptly let go of Thomas's hand. "Get in," she said when she opened the driver's side of a sleek black two-door car.

Thomas was still speechless. And humiliated.

After she started the car, she twisted to face him, then extended her hand. "Hi, I'm Janelle."

As he took her hand, she smiled . . . a real smile this time.

RETURN OF THE MONARCHS - CHAPTER 2

Thomas was embarrassed that a girl had to stand up for him, and he hoped Janelle would mistake his blushed face as being from the heat, not total humiliation. He kept his eyes straight ahead as he said, "I just live about a half mile from here. *Danki*—I mean thanks for the ride."

"Those guys are such jerks." She shook her head full of black hair as she shifted her car into gear. Thomas had driven an automatic car a few times. He was in his *rumschpringe*, or running-around period as it was often called by the English. But he'd never even been in a car like the one he was in now. It was a two-seater, rode low to the ground, and had all kinds of gadgets on the dashboard.

He didn't want to focus on what had just happened. "I've ridden by that store hundreds of times, but I've only seen an older woman out front from time to time."

"That's my mom. She's got an unseasonal case of the flu. She seems to get it every year, but usually not in the summer like this. So, I'm running the store until she feels better. I already work there part-time." She tapped her chin. "Depending on when I decide to leave for college, I might stay on and continue to help her for a while."

Now that he was seeing her up close, Janelle didn't look any older than Thomas, maybe even younger.

"How old are you?" he asked. "Don't you have another year or two of high school?" Even though Thomas's people only went to school through the eighth grade, he knew the English were usually eighteen when they graduated.

"I'm seventeen, but I graduated early." She turned to him and smiled. He wanted to ask her why she dressed in black. She wasn't wearing the type of black mourning clothes typically worn by the English.

"You must be really smart," he said as he glanced at her.

Janelle shrugged. "I don't know about that. I just didn't care for school and was anxious to graduate. It's a small town, and I never really connected with any of the kids over the past six months since we've lived here."

Thomas wasn't surprised based on the way she was dressed. He'd never seen any of the English kids here dressed the way she was or wear such dark makeup, especially around her eyes. "Where'd you move from?"

"Not far. Indianapolis. My mom grew up in the country, on a farm near Shoals, and she wanted to get back to her roots even though we don't have any family there or here in Montgomery. But Mom said Montgomery was a hop, skip, and a jump from her old stomping grounds, as she called them. My dad owns his own construction company, and after making some inquiries, he discovered there was plenty of work around here." She turned to him, her dark eyes taking on a glistening glow as she spoke. "My parents are still so in love after twenty-five years of marriage. I'm not sure my dad would deny my mom anything." She chuckled. "I still catch them making out like teenagers when they think I'm not around."

Her voice, ambitions, and sweet nature didn't seem to match the look she had chosen for herself.

"Go ahead. Ask me why I dress like this." She shrugged again as she cut her eyes at him, but with a grin on her face. "Most people are too afraid."

Thomas swallowed back a knot in his throat. He appreciated how candid she was, but wasn't it her business what she chose to wear? It wasn't an option Thomas could adhere to since his people all dressed alike.

"Uh . . . it's okay. I guess it's fine to dress however you like." He wondered if that's why she hadn't made any friends over the past six months. Close up, she looked like she might be pretty beneath the dark makeup.

"Wanna stop for a soda? I'm parched." Even with the air-conditioning blowing in their faces, the car hadn't had time to cool down. "My treat."

"That's *mei haus*, that way." He pointed to the road that led to his home.

"Soda or not?" She didn't slow down.

They passed the gravel road to his house. "*Ya*, sure." He didn't seem to have a choice.

She turned into the parking lot of a small diner about a mile further down the road, put the car in park, then exited the vehicle. Thomas stepped out and followed her.

Inside, Janelle ordered a root beer float, and Thomas

ordered the same before they took a seat at a booth in the corner of the small establishment.

"I haven't had one of these in a long time," he said as he slid into the seat and removed his hat. He took a long sip from the straw, absorbing a hefty chunk of whipped cream on top. "It's as good as I remember."

"My dad loves these. My mom can't stand root beer. It's one of the few things they disagree on." She smiled, and again, Thomas thought again about how pretty she would be without all that stuff on her face, but he also wondered if she had an explanation about her choice of clothing and makeup. Maybe he should have asked her when she brought up the subject.

She leaned back and stared at him. "I've seen you drive by in your buggy several times when I was helping my mom or just stopping by the store. Where's your horse and buggy?"

Thomas cleared his throat. He didn't like to talk about what happened, but it was a direct question he couldn't really avoid, especially if he wanted to find out more about her. "I got hit by a car. *Mei* buggy got pretty banged up, and *mei* horse is out of commission permanently, but she's okay. I'm on the lookout for a new horse, and *mei* buggy is getting repaired."

Her eyes were heavy and locked with his. "And you? Is that why you walk with a limp? I mean it's barely noticeable, but I just wondered."

Thomas focused on his drink and avoided her inquiring eyes. "*Ya*, I have a pin in *mei* leg."

She nodded. "People around here need to be more careful. Everyone knows the buggies have the right-of-way. If I had to guess, someone probably zoomed past you or spooked your horse to cause the accident."

"*Nee*, we were hit from behind." He flinched at the recollection, the crunching of metal against the back of the buggy, the way he was flung from his seat, landing on the gravel road, and the horrific moaning that came from his beloved horse.

"I can see you don't like to talk about this." She sighed as she pulled her eyes from his and took a long sip of her float. Then she leaned forward and found his eyes again.

He held her gaze even though it was hard to distinguish where the dark makeup started and ended since her eyes were practically the same color, a deep dark shade of brown, but with the shadowy makeup, her eyes looked almost black. He couldn't stand it anymore. "So, why *do* you dress like that?"

She grinned before leaning over for another sip, but kept her eyes on him, eyebrows raised. "You first." Her voice was soft and sweet, such contrast to her looks.

His eyes widened. "If you've lived here for six months, I would assume you know that we all dress pretty much the same." He scratched his cheek, surprised how much scruff could develop in one day. His father always said he'd have a fine beard when he was married and allowed to grow one. Right now, it was a nuisance to have to shave every day.

"Of course, I know you all dress the same, have the same haircuts, don't use electricity or drive cars, etc. What I'm asking is the same question you asked me . . . why?"

Thomas wasn't sure he'd ever had to explain this to an

outsider. "That's the way it is, the way it's always been. We follow the *Ordnung*, the rules of the Amish."

"I'm familiar with the *Ordnung* and the rules. But I'm asking for the meaning behind the rules. Why do you all insist on uniform clothing, houses, and everything else?"

Thomas had a feeling she already knew the answers to her questions, which made him wonder if she was setting him up for something. "There's no competition. We're all the same in *Gott's* eyes."

She smiled. "And there you have it . . . the answer to your question about why I dress the way I do. I'm not competing with anyone else. I don't care if other girls have fancy clothes, nor do I feel the need to fit in."

"You sure have a fancy car," he said, grinning.

She chuckled as she nodded out the window to the sleek black car. "Point taken. My dad bought it for me when I turned sixteen."

Thomas stared at her, waiting for more. When she didn't say anything, he asked, "I get the no competition, but why all black . . .?" He raised an eyebrow. "All black, even your eye makeup and fingernails?"

She looked down, her face taking on a blush for the first time, visible even beneath the makeup. "It's not for everyone."

"I didn't say I didn't like it." He didn't, but he didn't want to hurt her feelings. "It's just, you're pretty and you seem to be trying to cover that up."

Her cheeks glowed a brighter shade of red. She lifted her eyes to his. "I know it must seem like I'm hiding, but I'm not. I'm a future butterfly."

"Huh?" Thomas leaned back against the seat the same way she was and scratched his cheek again.

"I know people look at me funny. My parents think it's a stage I'll grow out of, and in some way they're right, but they're right for all the wrong reasons. I'm not being rebellious. I'm not a Goth chick or practicing devil worship and anything like that. I'm evolving, like a caterpillar before it becomes a butterfly."

Thomas was in over his head with this girl's reasoning, but he was intrigued by every word that came out of her mouth. "*Ya*, go on."

She took a deep breath, then held up her left hand. "See these two rings." She wiggled her fingers. The middle two had black rings, each with something silver atop them, something too little for him to see. "One represents the death of my grandmother and the other one the death of my grandfather." She paused, lowered her head for a moment, then added, "I don't feel at peace about their deaths yet. They both died last year, and I didn't get to say goodbye." She shrugged a little. "I will get past it, but I'm not there yet. I'll take them off when I feel peace about their passings."

She held up her right hand and touched a thick black band around her wrist. "I hit a wall in my bedroom when I was mad about something, and this reminds me that violence of any type should be avoided if possible. And until I can control my angry outbursts sometimes, I wear this."

Thomas could see where she was going with this, and he found it interesting, if not odd.

"The black clothes are because I am not the person I

want to be. I strive to be better, and as I grow and change, so will my clothes. And I believe all white should be reserved for marriage." She shrugged. "It's weird, I know, but it's how I feel."

Thomas gazed at her from across the table, trying not to scowl.

"You're staring at my face and wondering about my makeup."

He nodded. "*Ya*, I am."

She wiggled her mouth, covered in red lipstick, back and forth as she fidgeted with her straw. "I don't see the world clearly. I have questions. I want a better relationship with God. I want to understand myself better and what makes me tick. As I grow into the person I want to be, I will lighten my colors. And I feel that overall, about my appearance. I want to represent the version of myself that I see, and as I see changes—for the better I hope—then I will adjust the way I represent myself on the outside. And I don't worry about what people think of my looks or who they perceive me to be."

At some point, Thomas's jaw had dropped, and he was speechless. Although, everything she said made sense and inspired him to care less about the stares he received from the English sometimes.

"My parents aren't crazy about my choices, but they understood once I explained to them. I guess I haven't really made any close friends because no one bothered to get to know the real me. And that's okay. People shine from the inside, and I want to be friends with those who can see my light beyond my outward appearance."

Thomas wasn't sure anyone had shone more brightly in his eyes than Janelle did now.

"I think that's awesome," he finally said before he smiled.

"Really?" She tipped her head to one side before she leaned down and took a sip of her root beer float.

"*Ya*, really. I wish I was more like you. I worry too much about what outsiders think of me, the way I dress, and all the other things you mentioned. I admire your sense of freedom, and you know who you are."

"Not really. I mean, I know who I *want* to be, but I'm not there yet."

"I have a feeling you'll get there." Thomas couldn't stop staring at her, at the real person, the one she hid from the world. But he had one more question. "Why the bright red lipstick?"

Her cheeks began to turn pink. "You probably won't believe this, but I've never kissed anyone." She lowered her head before she looked back at him. "You know, a guy . . . like a real kiss. I'm seventeen so I guess that makes me a little freakish, huh? I'm sure even Amish guys your age have kissed girls by now."

Thomas hesitated since his people didn't usually discuss this kind of thing, but he finally nodded. "*Ya*, I have." Not a lot, but there had been a few. He had thought that each girl might end up being a future wife, or a girlfriend, but he hadn't met anyone that he'd gotten serious with so far.

She straightened. "So, when is your buggy going to be fixed? And you have to get a new horse, right?"

It was jarring the way she changed the subject so

quickly, but he was happy to move in another direction. "I don't know when either of those things are going to happen. I'm on the hunt for a *gut* horse, and *mei* buggy is being repaired now. Luckily, it's only a mile to work."

"And very unlucky that Brian and his goons live nearby. They will probably try to bully you again on your way home."

Thomas had been raised to be passive, but he didn't want to appear a coward to Janelle. "I can take care of myself."

She smiled a little. "I know you *can* take care of yourself, but I also know you don't want to, that it goes against what you believe in. And I lock up about the time you're walking home from work. Just come into the store, avoid those guys, and I'll drive you the rest of the way home."

Thomas felt like she was offering him protection from Brian and his buddies, and no matter how passive he might be, he possessed a certain amount of pride. But if he said no, he might not have an opportunity to spend time with her and getting to know Janelle better had suddenly become a priority. "*Ya*, sure, I guess that would be okay. *Danki* . . . I mean thanks."

She winked at him. "And maybe tomorrow we can change it up and get an ice cream sundae."

Thomas smiled. "Maybe we can." Then he winked back at her as he wondered what was happening between him and his new friend. Was she flirting? Was he flirting back?

He just knew he wanted to get to know her better, and a person could never have too many friends.

RETURN OF THE MONARCHS - CHAPTER 3

Janelle waited for the gate to open, then pulled into her driveway with a bounce in her step. Thomas was handsome, nice, and . . . safe. They'd never have a romantic relationship since he was Amish, so Janelle didn't have to dig into her deepest fears.

She went straight to her mother's bedroom since she'd noticed her father's car wasn't in the driveway. The door was open, so she tiptoed in, surprised to see her mother sitting up and reading a magazine.

"You look like you feel better." Janelle walked to the edge of the bed and sat. Her mom set the magazine aside and reached for Janelle's hand and squeezed.

"I do feel much better. How did it go at the store?" She yawned, covering her mouth with her free hand.

"Pretty good for a Wednesday Not much traffic, but two ladies came in and spent about a hundred and fifty dollars each."

Her mother raised an eyebrow. "Goodness. What did the ladies buy?" She gently eased her hand away, then tucked her shoulder-length blonde hair behind her ears. Janelle had always thought Sharlene Herron was the most beautiful woman and mom on the planet, inside and out. Maybe it was because she was an only child, but Janelle and her mother had always been close.

Janelle tapped a finger to her chin as she recalled the purchases. "Uh, let's see . . . the taller lady bought two books, three of the candles we had on sale, an angel figurine, and ten jars of jam, the kind Lizzie and Esther make with the Amish labels on them. And the other woman bought books, candles, and . . ." Janelle laughed. "And she bought that horrible red vase shaped like a shoe!"

Her mother's eyes widened. "You're kidding! I was sure we'd have to slash the price on that hideous thing to get rid of it." She shrugged. "To each his own, I guess." She glanced at the clock on her bedside table. "You're a little late today."

"Oh, yeah." She pushed dark strands of hair from her face. "I gave a guy a ride home."

Her mother frowned as she lifted a sculpted eyebrow. "Someone you know, I hope?"

She shook her head. "No, but he was an Amish guy."

"Amish have their own problems and bad eggs like everyone else. It's still not safe to pick up strangers, Janelle."

"I know, but Brian Edwards and two of his friends were giving the guy a really hard time. I watched out the window for a while before I went outside and got him away from them and took him home."

"Why does that name sound familiar, Brian Edwards?"

Janelle reached up and began taking off her black earrings, one pair at a time. Her mother frowned again, but she'd stopped commenting on Janelle's clothing and accessory choices a long time ago. "I think Dad knows his father. Brian is a real bully. I don't really know him, but I've heard stories, and today I witnessed it for myself. He shoved Thomas down, and I knew the poor guy wouldn't fight back."

Her mother shook her head, frowning. "Yes, an unfair advantage for Brian." She glanced at the clock on the nightstand again. "Where does he live?" she asked, clearly referring to the time again.

"Only about a half mile from the store, but we went to that little café and got root beer floats. Thomas is a super nice guy." Janelle liked the way his name rolled off her tongue, and she was lost in the memories of his blue eyes and the way he looked at her. When she snapped out of it, her mother was grinning. "What?" she asked.

"I think I saw some dreaminess in your eyes." She smiled as she batted her eyes at Janelle. "Is he cute?"

Janelle sighed. "Handsome, Mother. At our age, it's handsome, not cute. And, yes, he's very handsome."

"Be careful. He's Amish, and Amish only get involved with their own kind, at least most of the time."

"I know that we'll never be more than friends, and that's okay. I like him, and as you've said before . . . a person can never have too many friends." She half-chuckled. "And even one friend would be nice."

Her mother coughed, blew her nose, then said, "You do this to yourself, Honey. I understand why, but you are beautiful inside and out, though you never let anyone see the real you." She reached for Janelle's hand and squeezed. "Someday you will."

Janelle didn't think so, but she raised one shoulder and lowered it slowly. "Maybe." She felt more comfortable with Thomas than she had with anyone she'd met since they'd moved to Montgomery.

"I think I need at least one more day of rest, then I'll get back to the store. Are you going to stay on part time until you leave for college?"

"Yeah, if it's okay with you. I like working there."

"It's fine with me. I like having you around."

Janelle stood when she heard the front door close. She leaned over, kissed her mother on the forehead, and said, "Ditto," before she left the bedroom.

"There's my beautiful girl." Her father wrapped her in his arms the way he had her entire life. "My beautiful Goth girl."

Janelle sighed before she eased out of the hug. "Dad, I told you . . . no one dresses Goth. I'm just—"

"I know, I know. You're growing from a caterpillar into a butterfly." He rubbed her arm. "I'll be happy to see that butterfly when the time comes."

Janelle forced a smile before she inched around him and toward the kitchen. The whole caterpillar/butterfly thing was real, even though it sounded silly even to herself sometimes. But there was so much more to it.

Thomas took a seat at the dining room table across from his father while his mother and two sisters scurried around the kitchen. His siblings were probably trying to expedite supper so they could go meet their boyfriends down by the pond. Kathryn was nineteen, and Elizabeth was twenty, and they'd snagged two twin brothers—Abraham and Luke—who looked nothing alike. But the girls were smitten, and Thomas foresaw two wedding announcements in their futures. His sisters had been seeing Abraham and Luke for almost a year.

"What happened to your arm?" His mother frowned as she placed a butter dish on the table and nodded to the scrape on Thomas's forearm.

He glanced at the spot on his arm his mother was staring at. He hadn't even noticed the scratch, but it wasn't worth lying about. "Brian Edwards and two of his friends." Shrugging, he hoped that would be the end of it, but based on his mother's expression, she wasn't going to let it go.

Elizabeth gasped before his mother could question him. "Brian Edwards is a horrible human being." She slapped her hands to her hips. "He's a bully, especially to our kind."

"We don't speak that way in this *haus*, Elizabeth Marie." Lavina Schrock rarely raised her voice, and when she did, the family paid attention. "We don't call anyone a horrible human being." She pointed a finger at Thomas's oldest sister. "During prayer, you need to ask forgiveness for saying such a thing."

Their father cleared his throat. "*Ya*, well . . . if he's anything like his *daed*, he probably is a horrible human being."

His mother groaned. "Eli, you're not helping things."

His father shrugged. "It's true. I know who Brian Edwards is, and I've had dealings with his *daed*, a wretched and spiteful person. He often gets outbid on construction jobs—by me and others in our community—and he's been rather threatening about it. I'm sure that's why his *sohn* targeted Thomas."

"Are you hurt anywhere else?" Apparently, his mother was giving up the battle and refocused on Thomas's arm.

"*Nee*." Thomas shook his head as he reached for a slice of bread on a platter in the middle of the table even though everyone wasn't seated, nor had they said grace. He wouldn't eat it before they prayed. He just wanted to avoid the curious eyes that were waiting for further explanation. Passiveness might be the Amish way, but it was still embarrassing to not be able to stand up for himself when the situation warranted it. "It's just a scrape," he finally said.

His mother and sisters took their seats, and they all bowed their heads in prayer. Thomas thanked the Lord for the food and his many blessings, but he also asked God to keep Brian and his friends out of his way. It had been humiliating to be rescued by a girl.

"Where did this happen?" his mother asked, being the first one to raise her head to speak.

Thomas sighed. "*Mamm*, it's not that big a deal. Brian pushed me down, and him and his friends threw a bunch of rude comments *mei* way. That's all. And it happened across from that little store on *mei* walk home."

"Herron's General Store? I love that place. It's like a combination general store with gifts and food items."

"*Ya*, that's the place." Thomas began to fill his plate

with ham, potatoes, sweet peas, and cucumber salad, willing the conversation to be over.

"Sharlene Herron is a delightful *Englisch* woman. I've been in that store many times." She paused, scowling. "Did those boys give you a hard time the rest of the way home? That store is a half a mile from our *haus*."

Thomas laid his fork on his plate. "*Nee*, they left me alone, and Sharlene Herron's daughter was closing the store, so she gave me a ride home." *Now please let it go.*

"I've seen that *maed* working with her *mamm*." She paused. "She's very nice, like her *mudder*, but she dresses all in black. Even her face is painted with dark makeup." Tipping her head to one side, she waited for Thomas to look at her. "Did she say why she dresses so differently?"

Thomas sighed, frowning. "Why do we dress so differently?"

His father cleared his throat and shot Thomas a warning look. "Careful, *Sohn*."

Kathryn and Elizabeth were practically shoveling their food in their mouths, each glancing at the clock on the wall.

"Those boys will be down by the pond," his father said sternly. "Quit eating this fine meal as if it's your last."

His sisters grinned at each other before both declaring they were done.

"You will stay and help your *mudder* clean the kitchen, like always." Their father cut his eyes at each of his daughters.

"It's all right, Eli. Let them go." She turned to Thomas. "I'd like to talk to Thomas anyway. I don't get to visit with him as much as the girls since they're here all day and he's at work."

Thomas's father would retire to the porch where he'd read the newspaper for about fifteen minutes before he headed to the bedroom. His mother rarely wanted to visit with Thomas, so he figured it was about the girl from the store.

The girls wasted no time rushing to slip into their shoes while Thomas and his parents finished eating.

"And stay where I can see you out this window." Their father nodded over his shoulder to the kitchen window. Thomas—and his sisters—knew that their father could also see them from the porch and his parents' downstairs window. What they didn't know—or maybe they did— was that there was a patch of trees that blocked the view from all the rooms and porch. Thomas was sure that's where the kissing happened after his parents had extinguished their lanterns for the evening. Thomas had heard Elizabeth and Kathryn talking about kissing their boyfriends down by the pond. And it was bound to happen when they went on weekend dates where their father was nowhere around. He'd heard his dad say that he could control what happened on his own property and that he hoped his daughters acted respectfully, and Abraham and Luke too, when they were away from home.

Elizabeth and Kathryn were grown women, but Thomas believed that they acted appropriately, the way they'd been raised—his sisters and their boyfriends.

After his father finished eating and excused himself, his mother dabbed her mouth with her napkin. "What was Sharlene's daughter like? Did you get to talk to her much? As I said, she's always been very sweet, but I don't understand why she dresses the way she does." His mother set a stack of dirty dishes in soapy water, then tossed a dish towel over her shoulder and leaned against the counter, raising an eyebrow as she faced him. "Did she mention anything about that?"

"*Mamm*, does it really matter? She's just a girl who gave me a ride home." Janelle's admissions about her attire had felt personal, and he didn't want to share the information. "We stopped and got a root beer float at the café, and then she brought me home." He cringed when his mother rushed to the kitchen table and sat across from him, her eyes wide. Thomas shouldn't have mentioned that part.

"I saw a car drive away, but I couldn't make out who was in it. Even her car is black. Does she go to the local *Englisch* school?"

"*Mamm*, really? You're grilling me." He narrowed his eyebrows. "But I can see you're not going to let up so here you go . . . you're right, she's a nice person. Her name is Janelle. She's entitled to dress however she likes, and she offered to give me a ride the rest of the way home tomorrow, too, and I'll be happy to accept it since I'm dripping in sweat from the mile walk home. This way, it's only a half a mile." He took a breath. "And she graduated early before they moved here."

His mother rubbed her chin. "Where was Sharlene?"

"Her *mudder* has been sick, but I didn't get the impression it was anything serious."

She tilted her head to one side. "Be careful. There's nothing wrong with having a new friend, but just don't let it develop into anything else." She shook her head. "Although, based on her appearance, I don't see that happening. I think there's a beautiful *maed* underneath all that makeup, but I know she's not your type."

His mom stood and went back to the kitchen sink, seemingly convinced that Thomas and Janelle would never be anything more than friends.

But Janelle intrigued him, and he couldn't wait to see her tomorrow. He couldn't tell his mother his thoughts or that he couldn't stop thinking about her.

READ THE REST OF RETURN OF THE MONARCHS ON AMAZON.

AMISH RECIPES

Yumasetti Casserole

Ingredients:

 2 pounds ground beef
 1 onion, chopped
 12 oz. egg noodles
 2 cups frozen peas
 2 (10.5 oz.) cans cream of mushroom soup
 2 (10.5 oz.) cans cream of chicken soup
 1 cup sour cream
 2 cups bread crumbs, crumbled
 3 T. better, melted

Instructions:

 Cook the noodles as directed on the package;

 Brown the ground beef with the onion, then drain the fat;

 Combine the noodles, beef, peas, soups, and sour

cream in a large bowl. Pour mixture into a greased 9x13 baking dish;

Toss breadcrumbs with the melted butter in a small bowl, then sprinkled on top of casserole;

Cover the dish with foil and bake in a 350 oven for 25-30 minutes;

Uncover and bake for 15-20 minutes until lightly brown on top.

(Serves 10-12 people)

Onion Patties

Ingredients:
>
> 1 cup all-purpose flour
> 2 tsp. baking powder
> 2 tsp. sugar
> 1/2 tsp. salt
> 1/4 tsp. black pepper
> 2 T. cornmeal
> 2.5 cups onions, chopped
> 1 cup milk
> 1/2 cup cooking oil

Instructions:

Using a whisk, combine the flour, sugar, baking powder, salt, pepper, and cornmeal in a large bowl, then mix in chopped onions. Pour in milk and mix with a spoon.

Heat oil and carefully drop spoonfuls into hot oil. Cook on one side until brown, then flip to brown the other side.

Add additional salt, pepper, or other seasonings.

Pickled Eggs with Beets

Ingredients:
    2 (15 oz.) cans whole beets
    12 hard-boiled eggs, peeled
    1 cup water
    1 cup sugar
    1 cup cider vinegar

Instructions:
    Drain beets and reserve 1 cup of the juice;
    Put beets and eggs in a 2-qt. glass jar;
    In a small saucepan, bring the sugar, water, vinegar, and reserved beet juice to a boil;
    Poor mixture over beets and eggs and let cool;
    After covering tightly, refrigerate for 24 hours before serving.

Mae's Amish Chicken (Corn) Soup

Ingredients:
    1 cup shredded carrots
    2 celery ribs, chopped
    1 medium onion, chopped
    2 pounds chicken breasts, cubed
    3 chicken bouillon cubes
    1 tsp. salt
    1/4 tsp. pepper
    12 cups of water

2 cups egg noodles, uncooked

2 (14-3/4 oz) cans cream-style corn

1/4 cup butter

Nutmeg to taste (Mae's secret ingredient)

Instructions:

Combine first eight ingredients in a Dutch oven and bring to a slow boil;

Reduce heat and simmer, uncovered, until chicken is done and vegetables are tender, about 30-40 minutes;

Stir in the noodles, corn, and butter. Cook until noodles are tender, about 10-15 minutes, stirring occasionally;

Add salt and pepper to taste.

Hannah and Mae's Shaved Brussels Sprout with Nuts and Cranberries

Ingredients:

Cooking spray (your preference)

1 pound Brussels sprout

1/4 cup reduced sugar dried cranberries

1/8 cup pine nuts

1/2 teaspoon salt

1/4 teaspoon black pepper

1/4 teaspoon garlic powder

pepper flakes to taste (optional)

Instructions:

Pre-shaved Brussels sprout (or thinly sliced if not pre-shaved);

Spray a frying pan with oil spray and sauté the Brussels sprouts over medium heat until they start to soften, about 5 minutes;

Add the pine nuts and dried cranberries and sauté for another 2-3 minutes;

Season with salt, black pepper, garlic powder, and the optional red pepper flakes, if desired;

Remove from heat and serve right away.

Hannah and Mae's Candied Carrots

Ingredients:
    1 lb. carrots, peeled and sliced
    3 T. brown sugar
    2 T. butter
    1/8 tsp. pepper
    1/4 tsp. Salt
    1 T. parsley, chopped

Instructions:
    Combine 1 cup water and carrots in a large pot. Bring to a simmer, the cook for 8 minutes or until tender;

Drain the water, return pot to medium heat;

Add the brown sugar, butter, sale, and pepper;

Cook until butter and sugar have melted and carrots are coated in the glaze—about 3 minutes;

Sprinkle with parsley, then serve.

ACKNOWLEDGMENTS

My sincerest thanks goes to God for continuing to bless me with stories to tell.

Janet Murphy, you are an amazing assistant, marketing strategist, research pro, proof reader . . . wearing too many hats to list here. Much love and thanks for your keen insight about the industry, and especially for your friendship.

Much thanks to my dear friend and editor, Audrey Wick. I couldn't do this without you! Xo

To my sweet Hubby, Patrick, I love you. Thank you for the umpteenth time for doing life with me.

I have a wonderful street team who helps promote my books. You gals aren't just huge readers, but you are sincere, dedicated, and sweet ladies. Thank you from the bottom of my heart.

To Natasha Kern, thank you for setting me on the right professional path and for our friendship, which I cherish.

Thank you to my family and friends who continue to support me on this wild and fabulous ride. Love you all.

ABOUT THE AUTHOR

Bestselling and award-winning author Beth Wiseman has sold over 2.5 million books. She is the recipient of the coveted Holt Medallion, a two-time Carol Award winner, and has won the Inspirational Reader's Choice Award three times. Her books have been on various bestseller lists, including CBD, CBA, ECPA, and *Publishers Weekly*. Beth and her husband are empty nesters enjoying country life in south central Texas.

Made in United States
Troutdale, OR
11/15/2023

14602820R00076